FROM THE
NANCY DREW FILES

THE CASE: Emily Terner's high seas abduction leads to a tidal wave of trouble onshore.

CONTACT: Nancy attends a party at Emily's palatial house—but no one told her it would be an invitation to danger.

SUSPECTS: Seth Cooper—he'll do almost anything to win this year's regatta, and Emily is his chief rival.

Roland Lyons—the real estate developer wants to buy a stretch of untouched beach but is strongly opposed by Emily.

Keith Artin—Emily's ex-boyfriend tells her she'll get what she deserves, sooner or later.

COMPLICATIONS: The summer of love is almost over, and Nancy has yet to solve the biggest mystery of all—will she choose Ned or Sasha?

Books in The Nancy Drew Files ® Series

THE
NANCY DREW
FILES™

Case 50

DEEP SECRETS

CAROLYN KEENE

AN ARCHWAY PAPERBACK
Published by SIMON & SCHUSTER

New York   London   Toronto   Sydney   Tokyo   Singapore

An Archway paperback
first published in Great Britain
by Simon & Schuster Ltd in 1992
A Paramount Communications Company

Copyright © 1988 by Simon & Schuster Inc.

Simon & Schuster Ltd
West Garden Place
Kendal Street
London W2 2AQ

Simon & Schuster of Australia Pty Ltd
Sydney

A CIP catalogue record for this book is
available from the British Library

ISBN 0-671-71666-2

Printed and bound by
HarperCollins Manufacturing, Glasgow

DEEP SECRETS

Chapter

One

"NANCY, HELP ME!" George Fayne's voice was frantic.

Nancy Drew sprang forward and skillfully caught a plate full of nachos that was slipping from her friend's left hand. Then she surveyed the collection of snacks George was still balancing in her right hand. "Did you leave any food for the other guests?" she inquired with a dimpled smile.

George returned the grin. "*I* left a little, but Gary took everything else. Look at him—he's carrying three glasses of soda and two plates with only two hands. What a goof!"

Nancy laughed. George's boyfriend, Gary, was inching through the crowd toward the terrace,

1

hunched protectively over the food and drink he had collected. He turned to look at them and grinned, then twirled gracefully to avoid a girl's outflung hand.

"What a move! He should be dancing at the institute," Nancy joked. Her blue eyes twinkled as she moved forward to help Gary.

"Whew!" Gary greeted the girls. "When Emily Terner throws a party, she really packs 'em in! The people never end—and there are more out by the pool and down on the beach. I managed to find you two again, but I had some hairy moments. Here, have some food, everyone."

"My hero." George took the plates and glasses from him and set them down on a low table. Then, her dark eyes glowing, she planted a kiss on his lips. Nancy couldn't help smiling in delight. George and Gary were very much in love, and she was thrilled for them.

"A couple of the guys from Jetstream are here," Gary told the girls after they ate. Jetstream was the airplane-manufacturing company Gary worked for—he was a test pilot. "They don't know too many people, so I thought I'd introduce them around. Want to help out?"

"I'll pass," Nancy replied. "I'm happy right here, just looking at the moon and ocean."

George and Gary moved away to join Gary's pilot friends. Nancy leaned her elbows on the balcony of the terrace and let the gusty sea breeze ruffle her red-blond hair. What a gorgeous night!

It was Thursday, and they were at Emily Terner's palatial beach house, enjoying one of the last parties of the summer. A summer I'll never forget, Nancy told herself with a wistful sigh.

Nancy and George were staying with Nancy's aunt in the Hamptons, a group of exclusive Long Island, New York, beach towns. Usually Eloise Drew spent the summer at her cabin in the Adirondacks, but this year she'd switched houses with a friend. When she had asked Nancy, George, and their other friend, George's cousin Bess Marvin, to spend the summer with her, they'd jumped at the chance.

The summer had been incredibly exciting. The girls had been on the go constantly and had even solved a couple of mysteries. In fact, George barely knew Gary Powell when he was falsely accused of stealing plans from Jetstream. It had taken all of Nancy's skill as a detective to get to the bottom of that case.

Of course, it hadn't been all work and no play. The girls had also found time for quite a few beach parties, clambakes, boating trips, picnics, and nights at dance clubs. George had fallen in love with Gary, and Bess had found a serious boyfriend of her own, Tommy Gray.

And Nancy had met Sasha Petrov.

Nancy hadn't been looking for romance when she arrived in the Hamptons. She already had a steady boyfriend, Ned Nickerson, back home in River Heights. But romance seemed to have found Nancy, in the shape of a handsome nineteen-year-old ballet dancer from the Soviet Union.

Sasha was in the States to perform with an international dance company. Talented young dancers from all over the world had been invited to the Hamptons to take part in the two-month event. Sasha was one of the stars of the ensemble.

Eloise Drew was Sasha's official sponsor. That meant that Nancy and her friends often saw the dancer. Since they met, Sasha had been convinced that he and Nancy were *meant* to be together.

Nancy had thought he was just flirting, that his constant attention didn't mean anything, but Sasha had persisted. And these days, even though Ned was due to visit in less than a week, Nancy found her thoughts filled more and more often by a pair of intense blue eyes in a lean, high-cheekboned face. Sasha's face.

Am I really falling for him? Nancy wondered for the hundredth time. She picked up her glass and sipped, staring pensively out at the distant line of breakers glimmering in the moonlight.

"Hey, Nancy! We've been looking for you!" a girl's voice said. Nancy swiveled around to find Emily Terner. Emily's pretty face was wreathed in a smile. She held the arm of a tall, good-looking stranger. The guy seemed familiar, but Nancy couldn't place him.

"Emily! Hi!" Nancy felt her face break into an answering smile. Emily's perpetual high spirits were infectious.

"Great outfit," Emily said approvingly, taking in Nancy's silky white tank top and full white skirt that swirled around her slim legs.

"Thanks. Great party!" Nancy responded.

"Well, you wouldn't know it from the look on your face," Emily scolded her. "What's the matter—isn't Sasha coming?"

Nancy blushed. "He had a late rehearsal. I think he'll be here soon," she responded. "I was just . . . thinking."

"Well, stop thinking," Emily said. "Start mingling. I want you to meet Jeff. Jeff, this is Nancy Drew, the detective I told you about."

"Oh, no, what did she say about me?" Nancy asked in mock horror.

Jeff grinned. "Only nice things," he assured her. "But I was already sold, even before Emily started singing your praises. I want to thank you. You got my mother out of a bad situation."

"Your mother?" Nancy was mystified.

"Cynthia Gray," Emily explained. "Jeff's her other son."

"Oh!" Understanding dawned. Nancy had just solved a complicated case involving the art gallery Cynthia Gray owned. Among other things, the gallery manager had been cheating Cynthia out of large sums of money. Nancy had discovered the thefts and trapped the man into a confession.

"Well, you're welcome, I guess," she said to Jeff. "I can't take all the credit—I had a lot of help, and not the least of it from your brother, Tommy."

Nancy took a closer look at Jeff, then said, "No wonder you looked familiar—there's a strong family resemblance. I've heard from Tommy that you've been working in Maine all summer. Oh, he's dating my friend Bess, you know."

"I've heard, and I can't wait to meet her. Tommy hasn't talked about much else since I got home. I've never seen my little brother fall for a girl so hard," Jeff told Nancy.

"You should see the way Bess has fallen for Tommy," Emily put in, laughing. "You couldn't pry those two apart with a crowbar. Well, love is in the air these days. Right, Nancy?" She shook her thick honey-colored hair out of her face and gave Nancy a meaningful look.

Nancy felt an uncomfortable stab of guilt. Had her attraction for Sasha become that obvious?

An angry male voice broke in. "How would you know, Emily? You're so busy bouncing from guy to guy, you don't even have time to look around you."

Emily spun around. A muscular, black-haired boy with smoldering dark eyes stood behind her, glaring at her. Nancy recognized him—Keith Artin, Emily's ex-boyfriend. From what she'd heard, the breakup hadn't been Keith's idea. Uh-oh, Nancy thought. Trouble.

"Keith." Emily's voice was cold. "I didn't expect to see you here. Nancy, Jeff, you remember Keith, don't you?"

"Good to see you again," Jeff said, holding out his hand. Keith ignored it.

"Remember me?" He sneered, still looking at Emily. "You were hoping everyone would just forget me as fast as you did? Uh-uh, Emily, I'm not going to fade away that easily. You owe me."

"Owe you what?" Emily asked, taking a step forward. Her green eyes were beginning to flash with anger. Nancy tensed.

"Keith, chill out," Jeff said in a warning voice. He laid a hand on Keith's arm.

Keith shook Jeff's hand aside. "Don't touch me," he snarled. Spinning on his heel, he stalked away and disappeared into the crowd.

Nancy let out the breath she had been holding. "Well," she said, "I'm not even going to ask what that was about."

Emily shook her head. The color was still high in her cheeks. "He thinks he owns me," she said. "Dating him was like—I don't know, like being a pedigreed dog, or an expensive car, or something. No, I take that back; he spent more time on his car than he did on me. Anyway, I think it really took him by surprise when I broke up with him. It was like his chair had just talked back to him."

"He seemed pretty mad," Jeff noted.

"Well, he'll have to get over it," Emily said firmly. "Let's talk about something interesting. Like Roland Lyons and his condominium scam. Now, Nancy, don't look bored. I know I've chewed your ear off about this, but it is important."

"I'm not bored," Nancy protested with a grin. Emily had chewed *everyone's* ear off about Lyons. "I agree with you. But I don't think there's anything you can do. Lyons is going to build those condos whether you like it or not.

"Lyons is a real-estate developer from Montauk," Nancy explained to Jeff, who was looking lost. "He managed to buy up a lot of land surrounding this town—I think they call it a green belt—and now he's offering it to the community board in exchange for a strip of beachfront land. He wants to build condos. And Emily's dad says the board is going to go for it. They vote Monday."

"Roland Lyons is a crook," Emily burst out. "All he's doing is lining his own pockets—and ruining the most beautiful beach on Long Island!" She stamped her foot. "Someone's got to stop him."

"Emily, it's not a crime to make money in real estate," Nancy pointed out gently.

"Then it should be," Emily retorted. "And even if it's not, I'm positive Lyons is doing *something* shady."

"Like what?" Jeff asked.

"Oh, I don't know," Emily said impatiently. "But he's slime. He's got to be up to something. Once I find out what, Lyons had better look out."

"Wow! Remind me not to get on your hit list," Jeff teased. He grinned down at Emily, his hazel eyes crinkling at the corners.

"Be good and I'll cross you off." Emily smiled

back. It was a full-blast, thousand-watt smile, Nancy noted with amusement. Jeff didn't have to worry. Emily liked him a lot!

He looked dazzled. "Come on, let's dance," he said, grabbing Emily's hand. "Excuse us, Nancy."

"Have fun." Nancy laughed. Emily was right —romance really was in the air!

She craned her neck, trying to find George or Bess in the crowd. Bess was nowhere in sight, but Nancy finally spotted George's dark curls and crimson silk blouse down the terrace by another set of glass patio doors. She weaved her way through the crowd to join her friend and Gary.

"Have you seen Bess?" George asked, greeting her.

"I was about to ask *you* that," Nancy replied. "I'll bet she's somewhere with Tommy."

"No doubt." Gary grinned.

"Hey, I saw you and Emily talking to Keith Artin," George said. "I can't believe Emily invited him tonight. I mean, they just broke up!"

Nancy shrugged. "I'm not sure she did invite him. I think he just showed up."

George shook her head. "He never struck me as a very nice person," she said. "Cute, yes, and charming sometimes, but kind of selfish. I—" She broke off as a sudden commotion erupted from the far end of the terrace. "What's that?"

"I don't know." Nancy frowned. She could hear two male voices shouting at each other. "We'd better go see."

Nancy led the way through the party crowd. Music was still playing, but no one was dancing anymore. Instead, everyone was staring at Keith Artin, who was being held by two big guys in football jerseys. Keith was panting.

Across from him, Jeff Gray was sitting on the flagstone floor, rubbing his jaw. Emily knelt by him. She glared at Keith. "You jerk!" she cried.

"Turn me loose," Keith ordered the guys holding him. "Let go. I won't hit him again."

The two boys released Keith's arms. He walked over to Emily.

"This is all your fault," he said through clenched teeth. "But sooner or later you'll get what you deserve"

Chapter

Two

THE MUSIC ENDED just at that moment, and there was a tense silence. Keith stalked across the side lawn to his red sports car and drove away. As Emily scrambled up and ran into the house, Nancy saw tears in her eyes.

"Nancy!" A hand on her bare shoulder made Nancy turn around. Sasha stood beside her, his golden brown hair still damp from his after-rehearsal shower. "I just arrived. What has happened here?" he asked.

"It's complicated." Nancy smiled at him. His hand on her shoulder felt good. "George, can you and Gary see if Jeff's okay?" she asked her friend. "Come on, Sasha, let's find Emily. She's a little shaken up."

Nancy and Sasha weaved through the crowd of dancers. Someone had put on a tape, and the pounding bass rose above the hum of nervous chatter.

They found Emily in the darkened den. She was standing by a glass slider at one end, gazing out at the night sea.

"Emily?" Nancy said softly. "Are you all right?"

She made no response other than a long indrawn breath. Then finally she said, "Yes, I guess so. I'm just steaming mad at Keith!"

She stepped over and snapped on one of the lamps. Then she sat down on a leather sofa and gestured for them to join her. "Hi, Sasha," she said with a wry smile. "Fun party, huh?"

Sasha grinned. "It looked exciting to me," he said. "I think people will be talking about it for a long time."

"What happened?" Nancy asked.

"I don't know." Emily held up her hands. "Jeff and I were dancing, and all of a sudden Keith was there yelling at Jeff to keep his hands off me. Jeff told Keith to mind his own business, and Keith hit him."

"I didn't know Keith was such a violent guy," Nancy said, leaning forward.

"He has a terrible temper," Emily replied. "It was one of the things that made me break up with him. Once we had an argument—it was about Roland Lyons, in fact!—and he got so mad at me that he was practically foaming at the mouth."

12

"You had an argument about Roland Lyons?" Nancy was puzzled.

Emily sighed. "Yes. Keith worked for Lyons last summer, and he thinks the man's a financial genius—although how he could figure that out from mowing Lyons's lawn, I don't know. He thinks the beachfront development is a fantastic idea."

"Well," Sasha said cautiously, "houses around here are very expensive. Roland Lyons will probably make a lot of money. If you look at it like that, it *is* a fantastic idea." He shrugged his muscular shoulders.

Emily glared at Sasha. Then she turned back to Nancy.

"Look, I'm really fine," she assured Nancy. "I just need a couple of minutes to calm down. Go on back to the party—have a good time. For Pete's sake, I want *someone* to have fun!" She waved them out of the room.

"Nancy, let's walk on the beach," Sasha said. He took Nancy's hand and pulled her toward the terrace.

Part of Nancy wanted to go with Sasha, but part of her hung back. "I should find George and see if Jeff is okay," she said doubtfully.

"Jeff? The one who was hit? He was fine," Sasha said. "Come, walk with me. Tell me what I missed." He tugged Nancy's hand again.

A walk couldn't hurt, Nancy reasoned. It was such a beautiful evening . . . and Sasha's eyes were so blue. . . .

Ignoring the little pang of guilt, she smiled and followed Sasha down the terrace stairs to the beach.

The night was glorious. Waves crashed and foamed at the water's edge, and wind-whipped clouds raced across the sky, leaving ghostly shadow trails on the moonlit white sand. As they walked Nancy told Sasha about the events at the party, but after a while she noticed that he wasn't paying much attention. He was just staring at her. She stopped.

"Earth to Sasha," she said. "Have you heard one word of this story?"

Sasha gazed at her as if hypnotized. Then he reached out and gently smoothed a strand of red-gold hair off her brow. "You are so beautiful, Nancy," he said softly. "In your white outfit, in the moonlight, you look like a statue. But I hope you will not be cold and hard like a statue with me." His fingers trailed down her cheek.

"Sasha—" Nancy closed her eyes for a second. Her pulse was pounding wildly. The touch of Sasha's hand sent a thrill down her spine, reminding her of the moment a few nights earlier when he had kissed her and told her that he loved her.

That had been their first kiss, and Nancy had told Sasha that it would be their last, too. She'd told him that he shouldn't pursue her, but even as she was saying it, she knew she didn't mean it. Sasha knew it, too. So what could she say now?

How could she tell him to stop, when all she wanted was for him to kiss her again?

Suddenly Ned Nickerson's face swam before hers, his brown eyes full of hurt. I thought we could trust each other, he seemed to be saying. I thought you loved me.

I do, Ned, I do! Nancy wanted to cry out. But you're not here, and Sasha is, and—oh, why is everything so complicated?

She opened her eyes again. "I don't want to be cold to you, Sasha. I just don't know what I want," she told him, her voice trembling. "Give me time to figure it out."

"We do not have forever," Sasha said.

"Hey, you two, what are you doing out here?" came Bess Marvin's voice. She and her boyfriend, Tommy Gray, were strolling toward Nancy and Sasha, arm in arm.

"We were just on our way back to the party," Nancy said, glad for the interruption.

"Good, we can all walk together. Isn't it an incredible night?" Bess sighed. She twisted her long, windswept blond hair into a loose knot. "Look, there's a sailboat. How beautiful!" She pointed at some running lights and a triangle of white sail, barely visible. The boat was moving at a good clip across the choppy water.

Tommy peered out at the boat. "That must be Seth Cooper's sloop," he commented. "He's the only person I can think of who sails offshore at night. Alone, too. He's a terrific sailor."

"Cooper? Do I know him?" Nancy asked.

"Tall, gray-haired guy, probably in his early forties," Tommy replied. He grinned, a dimple showing in his cheek. "My mom says he's a hunk."

"Oh, I know who he is." Nancy laughed. "My aunt thinks he's gorgeous, too. He's new in town."

"That's him," Tommy confirmed. "He lives on his boat, doesn't socialize much. He seems like a good guy. As a matter of fact, he lost his crew and asked me to crew on his boat for the regatta."

"You didn't tell me that!" Bess exclaimed. She squeezed Tommy's hand. "That's fantastic!"

"I just talked to him about it yesterday. I hope my boss will let me have the day off." Tommy drove boats and rented out equipment for a water-ski rental shop in town.

"The regatta is Saturday, no?" Sasha asked.

"Uh-huh. And this year there are going to be some changes." Tommy ran a hand through his unruly blond hair. "Emily Terner has won hands down for the last three years, but I think Seth Cooper just might beat her Saturday. It'll be a race to see!"

A gust of wind blew Nancy's hair into her face. Lightning flashed, then came a rumble of thunder. "Oh, no!" she cried. "It's going to storm. Come on, let's run."

Laughing, the four teenagers raced back to the party.

* * *

"The wheels of justice are turning," Emily said, her voice loud to be heard over the rain thrumming on the metal roof. It was Friday, and Nancy, Bess, George, and Emily were sitting in a booth having lunch at Nino's, a local diner. "I called California this morning and spoke to Roland Lyons's old business partner."

"What about?" asked Nancy. She speared a chunk of tomato with her fork as a flash of lightning lit up the sky.

"I told you—I'm digging up dirt on Lyons."

"Shh! Not so loud," Bess whispered. "Isn't that him right over there?" She gestured with her head toward the counter.

Nancy turned. A slender, boyish-looking man with black hair and horn-rimmed glasses was sitting on a stool drinking a cup of coffee. He caught Nancy's eye and gave her a pleasant nod.

Nancy smiled politely. She had met Lyons once or twice. He'd struck her as being a little too fond of his own jokes, but that certainly didn't make him a crook.

Turning back to her own table, Nancy murmured, "So what did you find out, Emily?"

"Not much," Emily confessed, lowering her voice. "Mr. Berry didn't want to talk to me. All he would say was that he and Lyons split up on good terms. But I know there must be some reason why Lyons left California. I mean, why would anybody leave a thriving construction business and start all over again on the other side of the country—unless he had to?"

17

"Maybe he didn't want to get caught in an earthquake," George suggested.

"An earthquake!" Bess shrieked. "Really, George."

There was a clattering noise behind Nancy. Turning, she saw that Lyons had dropped his spoon on the floor. He picked it up, glancing over at their table again. Then he paid up and left, unfurling an umbrella.

"I didn't mean to shout," Bess murmured apologetically.

"Maybe Lyons was worried about earthquakes, but I think he was running from the law," Emily said doggedly. She glanced at her watch, then jumped up. "Oops! I've got to go," she exclaimed. "My dad's coming home—I want to be sure all evidence of the party is gone." She tossed a bill onto the table. "That should cover me. See you all later."

Nancy, George, and Bess lingered over lunch for another half-hour. When they paid their check and left, the rain was still coming down in almost solid sheets.

"This is awful," Bess moaned as they ran to take shelter under the awning of a hardware store down the street from the diner. "I hope they don't have to call off the regatta tomorrow."

Nancy glanced in the window of the hardware store. Roland Lyons was standing at the counter talking to Keith Artin. Nancy had forgotten that Keith worked there—it didn't fit in with his

18

rich-kid image. Nancy remembered that Keith's father insisted he hold a job.

"Look—Emily's two favorite people," she commented, smiling. "Good thing she isn't here."

"Yeah. She's probably home and dried off already," George said. A raindrop rolled off the awning and hit her on the nose. "Ugh! Let's go!"

The rain continued all day, with only a lull late in the afternoon. Overnight the wind rose. By morning it was practically at gale force. Nancy, Bess, and George drove over to Emily's house to see if she had heard anything about the regatta.

When Nancy rang the doorbell at the Terner house, the door flew open almost immediately. Mr. Terner stood there, looking as if they were the last people he had expected.

"Hi," Nancy said hesitantly. He was an imposing figure, stern and cold-looking, with silver hair. "We're friends of Emily's. Is she home?"

Mr. Terner sagged against the doorframe. "No, she isn't."

He seems to be ill, Nancy thought. "Is something the matter?" she asked.

"It's Emily." Mr. Terner sighed. "She went out sailing yesterday, during the break in the rain, and she never came back. And in this storm, she—" He paused for a painful moment.

"I think she may have been lost at sea!" he managed at last.

Chapter

Three

"OH, NO!" BESS EXCLAIMED.

"Mr. Terner, are you sure?" Nancy asked, aghast. "Did you call the marina? Maybe she slept on the boat or at a friend's house."

Mr. Terner shook his head. "I thought of that. I called the marina as soon as I realized she wasn't home. Her car is in the lot. And our boat, the *Swallow,* is missing from its slip." His hand on the doorframe was white-knuckled, Nancy saw. He was terribly worried!

"I'm sorry—you girls are standing out in the rain. Please come in," Mr. Terner said. He held the door open and the girls filed into the living room.

Nancy quickly introduced herself and her

friends. Then she got down to business. "Have you notified the coast guard?" she asked urgently.

"I've done everything," Mr. Terner replied. "Police, coast guard—I've called them all, for all the good it does." His nostrils flared with anger. "The police say it's the coast guard's job to find her, and the coast guard tells me they're helpless without knowing her speed and heading, and they haven't got the manpower for an adequate search. Incompetent fools!"

"I'm sure they're doing everything they can," Nancy said diplomatically.

Mr. Terner struck his fist against his other palm. "If only I didn't feel so helpless! All I can do is sit by the phone and wait!"

"Is there anything *we* can do to help?" George asked, her dark eyes anxious.

"We could ask around and see if any of her friends knew where she was going," Bess offered.

Mr. Terner looked taken aback. "Well, I don't know," he said. "Perhaps you could."

"Bess, that's a great idea," Nancy told her friend warmly. "Mr. Terner, we'd be glad to make some calls. We can also go down to the marina and see if the manager has any useful information."

"I don't know what to say." Mr. Terner's voice was gruff. "I'd—I'd be very grateful for any help you girls can give. Thank you."

"It's easy to see where Emily gets her take-charge manner," Bess commented as the girls drove through the pelting rain to the marina. "Mr. Terner was ready to seize command of the coast-guard station."

Nancy nodded. "I don't think he's used to needing anyone else's help," she said. They pulled into the marina parking lot. "Look, there's Emily's car."

Emily's silver convertible was one of the few cars in the lot. The top was up, and the windows were closed against the rain.

"What was she thinking of, going out in this?" George wondered aloud. The rain was gradually slackening off to a spitting drizzle, but the wind was still howling. The girls splashed across the lot to the manager's office. "I know she's kind of reckless, but this seems closer to stupid."

"George!" Bess looked shocked.

"George is right," Nancy spoke up. "And Emily isn't stupid. She went out during that lull yesterday afternoon. Something must have prevented her from getting back in." She tried not to think how serious sailing mishaps could get.

A moment after Nancy knocked, the manager's door swung open and a tall, bony woman in oilskins and rubber boots stood there. "You looking for me?" she asked.

"Are you the manager?" Nancy inquired.

"That's right. Name's Janette Hanks. What can I do for you?"

"We're friends of Emily Terner's," Nancy told her. "We were wondering if you could tell us when you last saw the *Swallow*."

Ms. Hanks looked regretful. "Poor child," she said. "I can't believe she did such a foolish thing. I thought Emily knew better than to go out in the dead of night in any weather."

"Dead of night?" Nancy frowned. "Her father told us she took the boat out in the afternoon."

"She did," Ms. Hanks agreed, nodding vigorously. "But she got in from *that* jaunt about nine-fifty last night. I watched her dock. I went home at ten, and when I arrived at seven this morning the *Swallow* was gone. Emily must've come back late last night and sailed out again."

"How could she have gotten out and then back in? Don't you lock the gates at night?" George asked.

"It's just a combination lock, and most of the boat owners know the combination," Ms. Hanks admitted. "Everyone knows that the last person out locks up at night."

Nancy shook her head in disbelief. It made no sense. Why would Emily do such a thing?

"Well, thanks for your help. Come on, guys, let's go home and man the phones," she said, turning to Bess and George. "Maybe Emily told somebody what she was doing."

Before heading home, Nancy stopped at a pay phone and dialed the Terners' number. Mr. Terner answered on the first ring. Nancy told him what Ms. Hanks had said.

"So she did come home last night," Mr. Terner said. "I thought I heard her car pull into the garage at about ten-thirty, but when I couldn't find her this morning, I assumed I had imagined it."

"Was she upset about something?" Nancy asked. "Has she ever taken off like this before?"

"Like this? You mean in a sailboat, in the dead of night? No." Mr. Terner's voice was angry, but then he paused as if to calm down. "I'm sorry," he said after a moment. "I know you're trying to help. The fact is, Emily and I did have—words. And she is a headstrong girl. But I assure you, no matter how angry she felt, she wouldn't risk her life just to make me sorry."

Nancy sighed. "I was wondering, why didn't Ms. Hanks tell you about Emily coming in last night?" she asked, changing the subject.

"Oh, I didn't speak with her—only her assistant," he replied. "I think I'll call the coast guard. Maybe they can use this new information." He didn't sound hopeful. "And thank you again, Nancy. I appreciate your concern."

Nancy hung up and climbed back into her rented car. The three girls drove back to Eloise Drew's house in silence.

"Aunt Eloise?" Nancy asked, opening the door.

"We're in here, Nancy," her aunt called from the kitchen. The scent of coffee wafted through the open, airy foyer.

"We?" Eloise must have a guest. Nancy was surprised—she hadn't noticed another car in the driveway.

The girls went into the kitchen. A tall, rugged-looking man with a thick thatch of iron-gray hair was leaning against the white counter, a mug in his hand. His piercing blue eyes twinkled, and he was chuckling at whatever Eloise had just said.

Eloise Drew was pouring herself coffee. A slender, elegant woman with shiny brown hair, she was a feminine version of her elder brother, Nancy's father, Carson. Nancy was struck by the resemblance as Eloise smiled a hello.

"Girls, meet Seth Cooper," Eloise said. "Seth, this is my niece, Nancy, and her friends George Fayne and Bess Marvin."

"Nice to meet you," Nancy said. Bess and George added their greetings.

"I nearly ran Seth down with my shopping cart in the supermarket," Eloise told them, laughing. "I brought him over for coffee to apologize."

"No apology needed," Seth put in. "If I'd known you were going to treat me so well I would have steered my cart into yours as soon as I saw you." His voice was deep and resonant.

Eloise's cheeks pinkened. "Oh, did you do that on purpose?" she asked.

"You bet," Seth answered, sounding serious. "I was so annoyed that the regatta had been postponed that I was looking for a fight."

Seth's words reminded Nancy of the reason they had dashed home. "Aunt Eloise, we're going to have to tie up the phone for a while," she said. She quickly explained about Emily and the *Swallow* being missing, and about what they were doing to help. Eloise was horrified.

"That poor girl!" she exclaimed. She turned to Seth. "You're the expert. Can she make it in weather like this?"

Seth shrugged. "I think you're worrying too soon. If Emily's half the sailor I've heard she is, she can ride out this storm."

"In this wind?" George protested. "Wouldn't the boat capsize and sink?"

"I doubt it." Seth shook his head. "I've seen the *Swallow*. She's got a good, heavy keel— probably about a forty-percent ballast– displacement ratio."

"What does that mean?" Bess whispered to Nancy.

"It means the *Swallow* couldn't capsize if you wanted her to," Seth explained, smiling. "The keel is weighted with lead. The ballast– displacement ratio is the ratio of the weight of the lead to the overall weight of the boat."

"Oh." Bess still looked mystified.

"So you think Emily's safe?" Nancy asked Seth. He must have sensed her skepticism.

"Don't get me wrong," he said. "I don't know your friend, but I've heard some amazing stories about her sailing abilities. Maybe this is one more hair-raising exploit. Maybe she's trying to prove something."

"Maybe," Nancy said, and let it go at that. A disturbing idea had just occurred to her, but she needed to check all the other possibilities first. "Come on, guys, let's start calling," she said to her friends.

An hour later they had called everyone they could think of who knew Emily, and they were no closer to finding the girl. No one had seen her the day before, either in the afternoon or in the evening. Nancy's feeling of unease grew.

"Well, that's the last person I can think of to call," George said as she hung up the phone. She sighed.

Bess's blue eyes were distressed. "This is so awful," she said. "Poor Emily!"

"What else can we do?" George asked.

Lost in thought, Nancy didn't even hear the question. George poked her in the ribs. "Hey, anybody home?"

Nancy jumped. "Sorry. I was thinking. . . . There are things that don't add up here. I just can't believe Emily would go sailing alone, in a storm, at night. And if she did, why didn't she radio in to ask for help?"

"What are you getting at?" George was staring at her friend.

"What I'm getting at is this," Nancy said. "I know there could be a lot of explanations. Maybe the radio conked out—although I remember Emily telling me they just replaced the whole system this year. Or maybe she got knocked out somehow or washed overboard."

Nancy leaned forward. "But I think we also have to consider the possibility that Emily has been kidnapped!"

Chapter

Four

BESS AND GEORGE stared at Nancy blankly for a moment. Then George shook her head.

"Wait a second, Nan," she protested. "I must be missing something. Did you say *kidnapped?*"

"What in the world gave you that idea?" asked Bess incredulously.

"I know it sounds weird, but just think about it," Nancy said.

"Look at Mr. Terner," she began. "Emily's the only family he's got. His wife died years ago, and Emily is an only child. His daughter means everything to him."

Nancy knew what she was talking about. Her own mother had died when she was very young,

28

and she and her father had a bond that was deep and special.

"Plus, Mr. Terner is a very wealthy man," she continued. "You both know that. I'll bet he could pay a lot of ransom money. Doesn't Emily sound like the ideal target for a kidnapper?"

There was a short silence. Then Bess cleared her throat. "Don't you think you're getting carried away?" she asked hesitantly. "No one's asked Mr. Terner for ransom money."

"Bess is right," chimed in George. "Honestly, Nan, I think you're reaching too far this time. Haven't you had enough mysteries for one summer?"

Nancy winced. "Maybe you're right," she admitted. "Maybe I'm looking for a mystery where there isn't one. But I still think there's something weird about Emily's disappearance."

The phone rang. Maybe it was a call about Emily! the girls hoped. Nancy and George both dived for it. Nancy got there first. "Hello?" she said breathlessly.

"Your phone has been busy for more than an hour," Sasha's voice complained. "I was just about to have lunch alone, but I would much rather have it with you. Will you invite me over?"

Nancy laughed. "Sasha, you're outrageous. Come on over. I've got a lot to tell you."

Bess and George went downstairs to rummage in the refrigerator for lunch. Before following them, Nancy called Mr. Terner. She asked him outright if he had received any ransom calls for Emily.

Mr. Terner was first astonished, then annoyed. "You've got an overactive imagination, young lady," he said harshly. "There's nothing mysterious about Emily's disappearance."

Nancy didn't think it would do any good to argue with him. "Sorry. I'm just trying to cover all bases," she said before saying goodbye. At least she had planted the idea. If anyone did contact him, maybe he'd let her know.

She ran down the stairs and into the spotless white kitchen, where George was putting together a huge shrimp salad. Bess stood at the counter slicing bagels. Eloise and Seth were gone.

"Mr. Cooper had to get back to his boat," Bess explained in response to Nancy's questioning look. "I think he made a conquest, don't you?"

"It did look that way," Nancy agreed. She snitched a shrimp from George's bowl and went to the window. The weather had finally broken and there were patches of blue in the sky. The sun was drying up the puddles on the flagstone walk.

As she stood there lost in thought, Sasha rode into view. Dismounting in a single motion, he unlatched the front gate and wheeled his bike toward the house. Nancy's heart beat faster as she took in his long muscles and lithe walk. He glanced up and saw her looking and blew her a kiss.

Nancy sighed and went to the door. What am I

going to do about him? she asked herself. I'm going to have to settle this—and I've got to do it before Ned gets here on Tuesday!

Clearly, right then wasn't the time. Nancy had more immediate things to talk about with Sasha.

Over lunch, Nancy filled him in on Emily's disappearance. Unlike Bess and George, Sasha was ready to believe Emily could have been abducted.

"It must be," he declared firmly. "She is rich, she is beautiful, she is an only child—and men like Mr. Terner always have enemies."

George snorted. "How would you know? You've never even met Mr. Terner," she said, but she smiled at Sasha as she said it. Even levelheaded George was won over by the Soviet dancer's charm.

"True, but I know his type. Cold, harsh, imperious. I have read about men like him in—"

"In your detective novels," Bess finished for him, laughing. "Right, Sasha?"

"Right," Sasha agreed with an undaunted grin. "I have learned much about America and Americans from my detective novels. Besides that, I know Nancy is not often wrong. Remember, I have worked on cases with her, too." He turned to Nancy. "What will you do next?" he asked.

Nancy hesitated. Sasha's enthusiasm made her doubt her logic. His talk about Mr. Terner's enemies sounded pretty silly.

"I don't see what I *can* do," she said at last. "Except keep posted on the rescue efforts. I'd like to stretch my legs now, though. Anyone want to bicycle over to the coast-guard station with me?"

"Not me!" Bess said promptly. "I'd rather go out to the beach. Maybe I can catch up with some of the people we couldn't reach on the phone this morning."

"I'll go with Bess," George said.

"I'll go with you, Nancy. Maybe we will find some clues," Sasha offered.

Nancy smiled. "Maybe," she said.

The day had become beautiful, with puffy white clouds blowing across a clear azure sky. Nancy felt her spirits soar. She smiled at Sasha, and their gazes locked for an instant in strong attraction.

The sun had dried most of the water on the road, but there was one stretch of sticky reddish mud where the road was torn up for repairs, right outside the town of Montauk, the farthest point out on the island. Nancy and Sasha dismounted and walked their bikes around the repair, but even so, Nancy got a long red smear of mud on her shorts from her bike's tire. She tried to brush the smear off, but it clung.

"Roland Lyons lives right there," Sasha said, pointing to a huge, modern glass-and-wood house set well back from the road. "See, his name is on the mailbox. You could ask him to let you clean the mud off inside."

Nancy grinned. "No, thanks," she said. "If he's half the villain Emily says he is, he'd cook us both for dinner. Let's just go on. Maybe there'll be good news."

But the visit to the coast-guard station was disheartening. The big switchboard sparkled with the lights of incoming calls. The busy petty officer on duty was polite, but it was clear that he didn't have much hope of finding the *Swallow*.

"We haven't had any radio contact," he explained. "Without any idea of where she's been or which direction she's heading, we've got practically no chance of finding her. We've put out the word to boats in the area, but there's not much else we can do. We're spread pretty thin at the moment. I'm doing double duty myself, answering distress calls *and* the phone. Excuse me—it's ringing right now."

Discouraged, Nancy and Sasha left the man frantically pushing buttons on the switchboard. Outside, a cloud hid the bright sun. Nancy shivered. Even though the sun came back out, the light was gone from the whole day.

"Well, it seems the battle is over," Eloise Drew said. "I just got off the phone with Dana Harding. She says the community board voted in favor of Roland Lyons's condo plan this morning. He signed the contract at eleven."

It was Monday, and Nancy and Eloise were on the deck in back of the house, relaxing in the sun. Bess and George were upstairs suiting up to go swimming, and Nancy was waiting for Sasha to finish rehearsing so they could go out in her aunt's small day-sailer.

"That's too bad," Nancy said sympathetically. "But I guess you knew it was coming, huh?"

"I suppose so, though there certainly were enough people here opposed to it. Not the people that counted, though." Eloise sighed, her brown eyes somber. "I keep thinking of poor Emily. She was so dedicated to stopping Lyons."

Nancy nodded glumly. It had been almost seventy-two hours since Emily had disappeared, and there had been no sign of her or the *Swallow*. It was beginning to look as if she hadn't survived the storm.

Nor had there been any ransom note or demand. Nancy felt awful for even having suggested it to Emily's father. In his anguished state, it was probably the last thing he had needed to hear.

A car horn sounded, and Nancy jumped up. "See you later," she told her aunt. Tying her tropical-print sarong firmly around her hips over her bathing suit, she ran down the front path.

Sasha was striding up the path, wearing red-white-and-blue bathing trunks, a T-shirt, and flip-flops. Behind him a car pulled away from the curb. Nancy could see Sasha's Soviet chaperon, Dmitri Kolchak, hunched over the wheel of the tiny compact. He stuck a huge hand out the window and waved a friendly greeting before driving away.

"Dmitri gave me a ride over. He is very jolly these days," Sasha said. "I think he likes America, though he would never admit it."

Nancy drove them to the marina; then they sailed out into Hampton Bay. She was at the tiller. Sasha had sailed only once before, so Nancy coached him on how to handle the foresail, or jib, while she took the mainsail.

He did well, though often he would neglect his job and stare at Nancy instead of the yarn "telltales" that told when the wind was flowing properly over the jib. After a while she started calling for a tack, or turn, every time she noticed him staring. Sasha caught on quickly and concentrated on his job.

They sailed in companionable silence for an hour or so, sticking close to the shore and heading upwind toward Montauk. It was when they sailed by a sheltered cove that Sasha broke the silence.

"Nancy!" he said urgently, pointing.

Nancy followed his finger and spotted the thirty-foot sloop, rocking on the tide with no anchor or mooring lines visible. Its mainsail flapped loosely in the wind, and the boat looked deserted.

"Let's get a closer look," she said. Dropping the mainsail so the little boat would lose speed, she guided it up to the stern of the sloop. She gasped as she read the emblazoned name.

It was the *Swallow!*

The boat's dinghy was gone—the rope trailed in the water. Nancy grabbed it and pulled herself up so that she could see over the stern.

A slight figure was sprawled unmoving on the cockpit floor. A tangle of honey-colored hair hid the face, but Nancy knew in an instant who it was.

Emily Terner.

Chapter

Five

NANCY BIT BACK A CRY when she saw that Emily's chest was moving. She was alive!

"Drop the jib and hold us in close, Sasha," Nancy commanded. Then she hauled herself over the stern of the drifting sloop.

"Emily!" she called softly. She shook the unconscious girl's shoulder. Emily's hair was matted, and her face was pale—even her golden summer tan seemed faded. She moaned, moving her head from side to side. Nancy gasped as she saw the ugly purple bruise on Emily's temple.

Sasha climbed over the rail and joined her. "I tied our boat to that extra line back there," he explained. "Is she all right?"

"I hope so," Nancy answered worriedly.

Emily's eyes fluttered open. "Where am I?" she asked weakly. Then she spotted Sasha and Nancy. "Where did you come from?" she asked. She tried to sit up, but Nancy gently pushed her back.

"Take it easy," Nancy cautioned. "You've had a rough time, from the looks of it."

"Emily, what has happened to you?" Sasha blurted out. "You look awful. Where have you been for all these days?"

"I wish I knew," Emily said, her green eyes darkening. "You'll never believe what happened," she added, glancing back and forth between Nancy and Sasha. She took a breath. "I think I was kidnapped!"

"What?" Nancy could hardly believe her ears. She had been right after all!

"Who—?" Sasha began excitedly, but Nancy gripped his hand and signaled him to be quiet.

"Start from the beginning," she commanded Emily.

"Well, I came in from my practice sail when the wind really started gusting, around nine Friday night. Keith was supposed to crew for me, but after what he did at my party, I didn't want him. So I was alone," Emily told them. "I guess I missed the race," she added, sounding regretful.

"It's been postponed until next week," Nancy told her, hiding a grin. If Emily was already thinking about the race, she must be okay.

"Oh, good!" Emily exclaimed. "I'd hate to have missed beating Seth Cooper.

38

"Anyway," she went on, "I cleaned up the boat and left the marina by about ten-fifteen. Ms. Hanks had gone, but she knows I'll lock up if I'm the last one out. I drove home and was getting out of my car when somebody grabbed me from behind and held this piece of wet gauze over my face. Ugh!" She shuddered at the memory. "It smelled sort of sickly sweet."

"Chloroform," Sasha said darkly.

"Probably," Nancy said. "Did you see the person who grabbed you?" she asked Emily.

Emily shook her head. "I didn't even know anyone was there. I tried to scream but the chloroform must have knocked me out."

Nancy nodded. "It works fast," she said.

"When I woke up, I was here on board the *Swallow*," Emily said. "I was in the cabin, and the hatch was bolted from the outside. The communications equipment had been ripped out, and all the portholes were sealed up and covered with those." She pointed to a pile of dark plastic garbage bags with bits of duct tape on them. "I probably should have left them on, as evidence, but I didn't think of that until it was too late. Anyway, a corner had come loose on one of them, so a little light came in. I could tell that it was early morning. And the wind was pretty high."

"I know," Nancy said, remembering Saturday morning, when Emily's disappearance had been discovered.

"Well, I banged on the hatch and yelled," Emily resumed, "but no one answered. Still, I could tell there was someone else aboard, because it felt like we were sailing a steady course."

Emily paused and put a hand to her head. "Boy, do I have a headache," she murmured.

"No wonder," Sasha commented. Nancy got a can of soda out of the cooler in her boat and handed it to Emily. Emily drank it thirstily and then continued her story.

"I don't know how long we sailed," she mused. "But finally we bumped against something that felt like a dock, and he—whoever was there—started mooring the boat. So I yelled some more, but no one answered. After a while whoever it was just walked away and left me," she concluded. Suddenly she looked startled. "How long *have* I been gone? I don't even know what day it is."

"It's Monday afternoon," Nancy told her. "You were missing all weekend."

"Everyone thought you'd been lost in the storm," Sasha added. "We began to fear . . ." He trailed off, but Emily understood what he meant.

"Daddy!" she exclaimed. "He's probably got the navy out looking for me. I have to tell him I'm safe." She struggled to a sitting position.

"Wait," Nancy said, holding out a restraining hand. "You can't do any active sailing with that bruise on your forehead. Sasha and I will do it—you just shout orders from here, okay?"

"Okay," Emily agreed with a shaky grin. "I don't feel so great, now that you mention it."

Nancy went on. "You haven't told us how you got that bruise—or how you survived, locked in the cabin for three days, or how you got out."

"There may be some evidence or clues to the identity of your kidnapper around here. If we know what to look for we may find out something," Sasha put in. His eyes were bright with excitement as he turned to Nancy. "Am I right?"

"You're right," Nancy acknowledged, smiling warmly at him.

With an effort she broke the spell of his gaze and turned back to Emily. "Just a few more minutes," she said apologetically. "Then we'll get you back in record time, I promise."

"Okay," Emily grumbled. "But I doubt you'll learn anything. I have no idea where the boat was moored."

"Just tell us what you do know," Nancy urged.

Emily sighed. "Okay," she repeated. "Whoever kidnapped me must've planned ahead, because he left me a week's worth of food— sandwiches, cans of juice, stuff like that.

"He was also nice enough to leave me a flashlight and some extra batteries," she went on. "There were a few paperbacks lying around, so I read them, and that helped pass the time. Being alone in that little cabin, in the dark, with no idea why I was even there—well, it was pretty horrible."

There was a brief silence. Seeing that Emily was upset, Nancy didn't push, but waited patiently until the girl could go on.

"The—the kidnapper came back a few hours ago," Emily resumed at last. "It was the same as before, no talking. I realized he was there when the engine started and woke me. We motored awhile, and after about half an hour he turned off the engine. Then he started unbolting the hatch."

"But I thought you never saw him," Sasha interrupted with a puzzled frown. "If he let you out, how could this be?"

"He didn't let me out," Emily replied. "He only undid the bolts about halfway. Then I guess he climbed into the dinghy and rowed away."

Nancy twined a lock of red-blond hair around one finger, her mind racing. The kidnapper had arranged it so Emily could escape, with a little work. Who would do such a thing, and why? This story was getting stranger and stranger.

"I finally got the hatch open, working from the inside with a butter knife. It wasn't easy! My poor wrist will never be the same," Emily said, rubbing it. "It felt like it took hours. By the time I got out, the kidnapper was long gone. And all that time, the *Swallow* was just drifting on the tide. For all I know, I could have been *anywhere* along this stretch of coast. And that's the story. Can we go now?"

"All right," Nancy agreed. She picked up the mainsheet. "I doubt we can learn anything more by staying here. You could have drifted miles.

Now, can you manage to steer while we raise the sails?"

"But, Emily, how did you get that big bruise?" Sasha asked as he fed the mainsail into a slot in the mast. It rose smoothly. "Were you struck?"

Emily looked sheepish. "Oh, that," she murmured. "I guess that's my fault. I was trying to sail back home after I got out. I was standing on deck, and before I could even get the mainsail up, the boom swung across and hit me on the head. Knocked me right out. That must have been just before you two came along and found me."

Laughing, Nancy took the wheel and turned the boat until it caught the wind. "We won't tell unless we have to," she assured Emily.

Emily returned the smile, but her mind had turned elsewhere. She didn't even notice that the jib was flapping freely.

"Trim the jib, Sasha," Nancy called.

Sasha saluted. "Aye, aye, sir," he teased. Then he turned his attention back to the sail.

With the wind behind them, they made excellent time going back. But Emily's preoccupation seemed to deepen the closer they got to the marina. She began to look quite nervous.

"Is something wrong, Emily?" Nancy asked her.

Emily started. "N-no, nothing's wrong," she answered after a minute. "Only . . ."

"Only what?" Nancy prompted. "Come on, you've been in a daze for the last half-hour."

"I've thought a lot about who might have kidnapped me," Emily said slowly. "And I guess I thought . . ." She trailed off again.

"You thought what?" Nancy urged.

Emily looked unhappy. At last she spoke. "Well, I keep coming back to one person. Keith!"

Chapter

Six

Keith Artin a kidnapper? Nancy shook her head. It was logical to suspect him. But why didn't it seem one hundred percent convincing?

"Is Keith a good-enough sailor?" she asked.

Emily nodded. "He's good, all right."

"Then I guess it could have been him," Nancy agreed. She nibbled doubtfully on her lower lip. "But there's no proof."

Emily looked even unhappier. "I hope it wasn't him," she said. "It's awful to think of anyone you've been close to doing something so—so sick, so senseless, just for revenge."

Nancy snapped her fingers. That was it—that was what was bothering her. "It *doesn't* make sense," she told Emily. "It's possible, of course—

Keith certainly seems like the kind of guy who would try to get revenge—but what happened to you doesn't seem like an act of vengeance. The whole point of revenge is that the victim knows who's torturing her and why. I'd think if Keith was trying to get revenge, he'd gloat about it. You said your kidnapper didn't. He was very careful to stay anonymous."

Emily brightened a little. "I hope you're right," she said.

"There are five or six people gathered at the marina," Sasha called back to the girls. "Emily, I think I see your father. Someone must have seen us coming and called him."

Emily's hand flew to her tangled curls. "I'm a mess," she said glumly. "I look like a kid. He's going to think this whole thing was my fault. Naughty Emily, making trouble again."

"Don't be so hard on him," Nancy protested. "You didn't see him the morning you turned up missing. He was frantic. If he acts gruff, maybe it's only because he just doesn't know how to show you that he cares about you."

Emily sighed. "Maybe you're right," she said. "It's just that he never does anything but lecture me these days."

Nancy nodded sympathetically. She could well imagine Mr. Terner lecturing Emily.

"We are approaching the slip," Sasha announced, sounding a bit alarmed. "Someone had better tell me what to do next."

The girls burst out laughing. "Sorry we left you in the lurch!" Emily called.

For the next few minutes the three of them were too busy maneuvering the *Swallow* into her slip to greet anyone. But as soon as Nancy had the operation under control, Emily hurried to the bow and climbed over the rail onto the dock.

Her father stood in front of a small crowd, his face still showing the lines of strain. "Thank goodness!" he said in a hoarse voice. He held out his arms, and for a long moment father and daughter hugged silently. A cheer went up from the people who had gathered to watch the *Swallow*'s return.

"Okay, folks, let these people have some privacy," Ms. Hanks ordered. "We'll get the story soon enough."

Mr. Terner held Emily at arm's length. "Where have you been?" he demanded. Then, as Emily bristled at the implied reproach, he passed a hand over his face. "Never mind. Tell me later. I'm just glad you're safe."

"But, Daddy, it wasn't my fault this time!" Emily cried. She appealed to Nancy. "Tell him."

Nancy checked the mooring lines to make sure they were tight, then joined the Terners. Sasha was right behind her. "It's true, Mr. Terner," she said. The crowd was dispersing, but she spoke in a low voice so that no one would overhear. "I don't understand quite what happened, or why, but someone kidnapped Emily."

"What?" Mr. Terner looked from Nancy to Emily in disbelief. "Is this some kind of joke?"

"No!" Emily replied earnestly. "It's all true!" In an undertone, she told him the same story she had just told Nancy and Sasha.

When Emily finished talking, Mr. Terner drew a long breath. "Well," he said, sounding a little dazed, "this is incredible. We'll have to report it to the authorities right away."

"You believe me?" Emily asked incredulously.

Mr. Terner gave her a rueful look. "You're my daughter. You deserve my trust. I'm sorry I don't always seem to remember that."

He turned to Nancy. "And I apologize for not taking you seriously, Nancy," he said. "It seems you were right all along."

Nancy shook her head. "Don't thank me," she said sincerely. "This wasn't at all what I was thinking of. I don't understand this kidnapping. Why would anyone not ask for ransom?"

"Let's hope the police can find the answer to that," Mr. Terner replied. "Ready, Emily?"

"In a second—I'll meet you at the car," Emily told him. Taking Nancy's arm, she steered her over to the edge of the dock. "I'm borrowing Nancy for a minute," she called to Sasha.

"What's up?" Nancy asked, smiling. Emily looked worried.

"I'd rather not tell the police anything about Keith," Emily said. "I know he's a jerk and everything, but I don't want to accuse him of anything unless I *know* that it's possible."

"And so—?" Nancy prompted her.

"So I was hoping you'd poke around for me to see if you can find out anything one way or the other," Emily said slowly.

Nancy thought it over. "Okay," she said at last. "You know I think it's unlikely that it's Keith, but I may find something you won't like."

"I know." Emily nodded somberly. The squawk of her father's car horn made her jump just then. She squeezed Nancy's arm and hurried away.

Deep in thought, Nancy walked back to Sasha. "What was that about?" he asked curiously.

Nancy hesitated only a moment before telling him. She'd need his help, and Bess and George's as well, if she was going to run an investigation.

When she told him about Emily's initial suspicions about Keith, Sasha rubbed his hands. "Well, where do we start? Shall we use—what do you call it?—'shock tactics' and confront Keith?"

"No," said Nancy decisively. "We won't look for evidence against Keith specifically. That wouldn't be fair. We've got to look for any and all clues, and *then* see what kind of conclusions we can draw from the evidence. Let's start by searching the cabin of the *Swallow*."

Sasha brushed the curve of Nancy's cheek with his fingertips. "I find smart girls attractive," he murmured, a roguish grin crossing his face.

"Keep your mind on your work, Mr. Petrov," Nancy scolded, and led him aboard the *Swallow*.

There was nothing much in the cabin, though. They found wrappers from Emily's sandwiches and some empty juice cans, which the police would have to check for fingerprints, but Nancy doubted there would be any, other than Emily's. Whoever was behind this was too smart to leave prints.

Nancy also found the flashlight and batteries that the kidnapper had left for Emily. She was disappointed to see that both were common brands. They looked new, but no one would remember who bought them—hardware stores and drugstores must sell dozens like them every day. Still, it would all have to be checked out.

"Let's look around the deck," she suggested to Sasha. "That's where the kidnapper was last."

They went topside, and Nancy clambered up onto the foredeck. Near the prow, she found a smudge of light, pinkish brown mud on the white fiberglass. Now, what did that mean? she mused. It had to have been made after the last rain, which was Saturday. Neither she nor Sasha had been on the foredeck, so they couldn't have made it.

"Big deal," she said aloud. She was feeling frustrated. Even if the kidnapper had made the smudge, what did it tell her? Probably everyone on Long Island had muddy shoes after the bad weather they'd had Friday and Saturday.

Nancy glanced at her watch. It was five o'clock. She jumped down into the cockpit. "Find anything?" she asked Sasha. He shook his head.

"Let's go, then," she said. "I don't think we'll find any more clues here. And I've got to get home—I'm supposed to cook dinner tonight."

They docked Eloise's boat; then Nancy drove Sasha back to the house where the Soviet dancers were staying. She raced home to start the grill on the patio. Her aunt had left a note saying she wouldn't be home for dinner, but Bess and George would be. As she skewered the chicken pieces she had marinated that morning, adding cherry tomatoes, onions, and mushrooms, Nancy told her friends about the afternoon's adventure.

When she finished, Bess let out a long breath. "I can't believe it," she exclaimed. "Nan, you were right all along,"

George unbent her long legs from a runner's stretch—she had just come in from jogging on the beach. "Do you really think Keith could have done it?" she asked skeptically.

"I don't know. It feels wrong to me," Nancy admitted. "But I can't think of anyone else with a better motive. This whole case makes no sense." She jabbed a skewer into the last piece of chicken and put it on the grill.

"What do we do next?" George wanted to know.

"I guess we should talk to Keith," Nancy replied. "I'd rather have some evidence first, but I don't know where else to start looking."

"Mmm, that smells fantastic," Bess said. "I'll

set the table. Let's worry about the case after dinner."

As they ate, Bess chattered about how much fun she and George had had swimming. But Nancy had trouble keeping her mind on what her friend was saying. She kept thinking about the case. Who might have kidnapped Emily, and why? Was it to get her out of the way? Out of the way for what?

Nancy was carrying her plate to the kitchen when she heard a car screech to a stop in front of the house. Seconds later someone was pounding on the front door.

Nancy hurried to the door and flung it open. Emily Terner ran in, frantic.

"Emily, what's the matter?" Nancy cried.

"Keith," Emily gasped. "He had an accident. In his car."

Nancy's heart sank. "How bad?" she asked.

"Bad." Emily drew a deep breath. "He's in the hospital. Nancy, the doctor says he might not make it!"

Chapter

Seven

BESS GASPED. She and George had come in from the kitchen and had heard the whole thing.

Emily burst into tears. Nancy led her to a chair. "Shh. Just sit until you feel better," she advised Emily.

Emily took a tissue from the box Bess held out and blew her nose. "I'm sorry," she said, sniffling. "It's just such a shock—"

"Of course it is," George said.

"Do you feel like telling us what happened?" Nancy asked gently.

Emily nodded, swallowing hard. "His mom told me," she explained. "Poor Mrs. Artin, she's a wreck. So am I—this day has been too much."

"Take it easy," Bess said soothingly.

"Keith was in Montauk. He took the day off from work, I guess," Emily explained. "He was on his way home, and he lost control of his car on a sharp curve. It went off the road and flipped over. Keith was unconscious when they got him out, and he's in a coma now."

Nancy winced. That was pretty bad.

"I called his house because I wanted to ask him about the kidnapping." Emily looked ready to cry again. "I feel awful. What if he dies?"

"He won't," Bess said stoutly. She handed Emily the tissues. "He'll pull through."

"Bess is right," Nancy put in. "He's young and strong. He'll make it."

Emily began to look a little less stricken. "I hope you're right." She wadded the damp tissue into a ball. "You know, I felt so guilty when I heard. All I could think of was that I was going to accuse Keith of an awful crime, and there he was fighting for his life in the hospital."

Nancy went into the kitchen and came back with four glasses of lemonade. "We still can't rule out Keith as a suspect," she said.

"But how can you question him if he's in a coma?" George protested.

"We'll have to start somewhere else," Nancy said.. "Emily, what do the police think?"

Emily grimaced. "Not much. They're investigating, but the officer who took my statement said there wasn't much to go on."

"Let's think about it for a minute," Nancy suggested. "Usually people are kidnapped for ransom. But no one asked for any money in your case. Now, why else would anyone want to kidnap you?"

"Maybe someone wanted to put pressure on my father," Emily suggested. "One of his competitors in business or something like that."

"Maybe—but, again, no specific demands were made. How could your father know what he was being pressured about?" Nancy asked.

"It's got to be revenge," George said. "And that means it's got to be Keith."

"Not so fast," Nancy said, frowning as she thought. "I just came up with one other motive. What if someone wanted to get you out of the way for a particular period of time?"

"You mean, like in the movies when they kidnap the heiress so she can't claim her million-dollar inheritance?" Emily asked.

Nancy laughed. "Something like that. Now, what happened this past weekend?"

"I was *supposed* to work on my tan," Bess quipped. "But it rained. Hey! The regatta! It was supposed to be Saturday. It was postponed because of the weather, but no one knew for sure that it would be until Saturday morning."

"That's right! And, Emily, you were expected to win," George said excitedly. "Maybe someone wanted to get you out of the way."

"Someone—like Seth Cooper?" Nancy mused. She frowned, thinking of Seth's annoyance over the race being postponed. How serious had he been? Could he have wanted to ensure his victory by removing the closest competitor? "He's got the skill to have pulled it off," she said aloud. "We know he's a great sailor."

"I doubt that he'd do anything like that," Emily said. "Sailors don't go in much for dirty tricks."

"Well, what about money?" George suggested. "Isn't there a silver trophy for the winner?"

Nancy shook her head. "It's small and isn't worth much. Besides, if the kidnapper wanted money, he would have asked for ransom."

"Hey!" Emily cried, jumping to her feet. "Roland Lyons! I heard he signed the condo contract this morning. He could have wanted me out of the way until the deal was done. We all know he's a crook. Why didn't I think of him before?"

Nancy felt a little exasperated with Emily. She was taking the Lyons thing too far!

"Emily, you couldn't have stopped the deal from going through," she said patiently. "Lyons knew he had it. Why would he risk everything by kidnapping you, if he didn't need to?"

"Maybe I *could* have stopped it," Emily insisted. "I was digging into his past. Maybe he does have some secrets he'd rather not tell."

"Maybe." Nancy let it go at that. She didn't want to argue right then. Her brain was tired. It had been a long day.

"I say we forget about everything until tomorrow and watch a movie instead," Bess declared. "Tommy and I were going to rent something fun. We could make it a party."

"That sounds great," Nancy said, smiling.

"I'm going to invite Gary." George picked up the phone. "I'll ask him to bring some soda."

Emily looked regretful. "I've got to go home. My dad's expecting me," she said.

Nancy thought that sounded promising. Maybe things were better between Emily and her father.

As she walked Emily out to her car, Nancy thought of something. "Emily, I'd like to try to find the place where your kidnapper hid the *Swallow,*" she said. "It might tell us something about who did it. Can you come out sailing tomorrow? Maybe we'll be able to jog your memory somehow."

"If you think it'll help, sure," Emily replied. "And, Nancy, thanks for everything you've done so far." She gave Nancy a quick hug and climbed into her car. "See you tomorrow—at the marina around lunchtime?"

Nancy wandered around to the back of the house. The next day was going to be a busy one. She wanted to check out the flashlight and batteries with the area drugstores and hardware stores. That would take a while. Also she'd made plans to go sailing with Emily, and Ned was coming, and—

Oh, no! It had totally slipped her mind.

Nancy rushed into the big living room. George looked up from the video catalog she and Bess were studying. "Are you going to invite Sasha over?" she inquired.

"You guys, Ned's coming tomorrow. How could I have forgotten?" Nancy cried.

George raised her eyebrows. "Well, you have had a few things on your mind," she drawled.

"What's the big deal?" Bess asked. "You remembered in time."

"I know, I know. I'm just not—oh, I can't explain it," Nancy said lamely. How could she describe the turmoil in her feelings?

Bess spoke up again. "We know what you mean," she said softly. "Anyone with eyes in her head can see the way you light up when Sasha's around."

"It's that obvious?" Nancy asked, distressed.

Bess and George nodded in unison.

"What are you going to do?" George asked.

Nancy shook her head. "I don't know what I want anymore. Sasha's so alive, so—"

"So gorgeous," Bess supplied helpfully.

"So gorgeous," Nancy agreed with a wry grin. She flopped down on the sofa, hands in the pockets of her baggy blue jeans. "But Ned is those things, too, and more."

"I wouldn't know who to choose," Bess said. "They're both great guys."

"Remember, Nan, Sasha's leaving the country in a few weeks," George put in.

"Yeah, but Ned goes back to college in a few weeks, and that's almost as bad," Bess added.

"Thanks for the point-counterpoint." Nancy laughed. "Score one for each guy."

The doorbell rang, and Bess flew to answer it. They heard Tommy's voice in the foyer.

George grinned. "You're welcome. But seriously, they're both great. You just have to figure out who's right for *you.*"

"I know." Nancy sighed. Unfortunately, that was easier said than done.

Nancy got up at ten the next morning and dragged herself into the shower, feeling as if she'd barely slept at all. Between thinking about the case and worrying about Ned and Sasha, she'd tossed and turned all night. She'd been awake when her aunt Eloise had come in at one-thirty in the morning. Since she'd overslept, she decided, the flashlight investigation would have to wait until the next day.

Eloise looked wide-awake and cheerful that morning, though. "Morning," Nancy greeted her aunt. "Where were you so late last night?"

"I had dinner with Seth Cooper, and then we went to the movies," Eloise replied.

"Really! Did you have fun?" Nancy gave Eloise a sidelong look. If her aunt was falling for one of the suspects, there could be trouble.

"Mmmm. It was nice." Eloise's voice was casual, but her glowing eyes gave her away. She'd had a great time.

"Bess and George are already out on the beach," Eloise said. "They said they'd be back before lunch. Ned will be here soon, won't he?"

"Yes," Nancy mumbled. Very soon, in fact. His flight was due in at the East Hampton airport at eleven. She'd have to hurry to meet his plane.

Nancy arrived at the airport just as Ned's plane was taxiing down the runway. It pulled up in front of the small terminal, and a ground crew wheeled some steps into place.

Nancy drew a deep breath and went to the door of the terminal. Her stomach was doing flips.

But when the door opened and she found herself looking into her boyfriend's warm brown eyes and basking in his joyous smile, her worries suddenly seemed less urgent. It was so good to see him!

"Ned!" she cried, throwing her arms around him. A tingle went down her spine as he crushed her in a bear hug. Then when he kissed her, she forgot everything except the wonderful feeling of his lips, warm on hers.

"That's got to be the best welcome I've ever had," he told her when their lips finally parted.

"I'm so glad you're finally here," she replied, and meant it. "Come on, let's go home."

At the house Nancy showed Ned to a small spare room. They had just finished a tour of the house when Bess and George came back from the beach.

They greeted Ned enthusiastically, though George gave Nancy a questioning look over her shoulder. Nancy shrugged and smiled.

"Shouldn't we be going to Emily's soon?" George asked after a few minutes.

Nancy looked at her watch. "That's right! Um, Ned, I should have told you sooner, but—"

Ned groaned. "You don't have to say it. I can guess. You're on another case, right?"

She nodded guiltily.

"I should have known. Another vacation, another mystery," he complained in an exaggerated moan. He grinned at Nancy's anxious expression. "Let's go. You can tell me about it in the car."

Nancy blew him a kiss. "You're the greatest," she said. "And you're dressed for sailing!"

The phone rang as they were heading out the door. "Go on out to the car. I'll get it," Nancy said, as she picked up the phone. "Hello?"

"Nancy, we must talk."

"Sasha!" His voice sent a jolt through Nancy. "Uh, can it wait? I'm on my way out."

For once Sasha sounded deadly serious. "I cannot wait much longer for you. I have a decision to make."

"Decision? What do you mean?" Nancy asked.

There was a long silence. Then Sasha spoke up. "I have been offered the chance to stay in America and dance for a whole year. But it depends on you. Do you want me to stay, Nancy Drew?"

Chapter

Eight

Nancy felt as though she couldn't breathe properly. "Sasha, I—"

Outside, Ned honked the horn impatiently. Nancy suddenly realized she was keeping them all waiting. "I can't talk about this right now," she said desperately. "I'm sorry."

"When, then?" Sasha pressed. "Or are you too busy, now that Ned is here?"

"No!" Nancy cried, hurt. "I don't know— maybe tomorrow. He just arrived, Sasha. What do you want me to do?"

"That is your decision. I'll see you tomorrow." Sasha hung up.

Nancy leaned against the front door for a second before opening it. Then she walked down to the car. Five minutes ago everything had seemed so clear and simple! But now—now it just felt impossible. What am I going to do? she wondered.

"Who called?" Bess asked as Nancy slid into the driver's seat.

"Oh—it was for Aunt Eloise," Nancy said. The minute the words were out of her mouth, she wondered why she'd lied. Ned knew she was friendly with Sasha. Why not tell the truth?

"Are you okay?" Ned asked her, reaching over and squeezing her hand.

"Huh? Oh—oh, sure, I'm fine," Nancy stammered. Snap out of it! she admonished herself.

"Good," Ned said heartily, but Nancy noticed that he gave her an odd look out of the corner of his eye.

Nancy was glad to let Bess and George tell Ned about the case as they rode to the marina. It gave her the chance to think the situation over. She managed to calm down a little, but once or twice she noticed Ned giving her those strange sidelong glances. He knows me too well, she realized. He knows something's up.

When they arrived, Emily was waiting for them beside her car. Nancy introduced her to Ned.

"Nice to meet you," Emily said, shaking Ned's hand.

"Likewise." Ned grinned. "I've heard a lot about you in the last ten minutes."

Emily returned his grin cockily. Nancy

couldn't help smiling as she watched the two of them. Emily looked like a child next to Ned, her petite frame dwarfed by his six-foot-two height and broad shoulders.

"I hope I won't be ruining your vacation by dragging you around on a search for clues," Emily was saying. "At least I can promise you a picnic lunch on board a decent sailboat."

"What more could I want?" Ned said, spreading out his hands. "It sounds great."

"Let's go, then," Emily said. She hefted a huge wicker picnic basket. "You carry this."

Everyone laughed. "Take-charge Emily," Bess said admiringly.

Nancy's eyes followed Ned as he strode down the dock at Emily's side. Just as they reached the *Swallow*'s slip, he turned and met her gaze with a long, questioning look. Then he turned again and climbed aboard the sloop.

This isn't fair to Ned, Nancy thought. I have to tell him what I'm thinking. I owe him that. I'll talk to him the first chance I get.

Feeling better, she clambered over the deck rail and dropped into the cockpit. "Set the course, cap'n," she told Emily.

The day was perfect, with a wind that made sailing as easy as walking. Emily steered, Bess and George tended the mainsail, and Ned and Nancy each took one of the jib lines.

Nancy had learned most of what she knew about sailing from Ned—his family had a cabin on a lake, and they'd done some boating there.

But George and Bess had hardly sailed before the beginning of the summer.

"Here's a little sailing lesson for you landlubbers," Emily said, adopting a gruff, commanding tone of voice. "We're sailing on a 'beam reach.' That means the wind is blowing straight across the boat. Also, the wind is coming over the port side, which puts us on a starboard tack. That's good—it means we have the right-of-way. Everyone else has to get out of our way."

"Sounds good to me," Bess said. "I don't think I'd know how to dodge another boat."

"Now that we've set the sails and we're heading in the right direction, no one really has to do much—except for Ned," Emily continued, grinning at him. "He's on the starboard jib sheet, and we're on a starboard tack, so he's got what we call the 'working' jib line. Ned, you've got to keep an eye on the jib and make sure it never loses the wind. All right?"

Ned saluted. "Aye, aye, skipper."

Nancy stretched out her long legs. "And don't you slack off," she ordered her boyfriend with a grin.

So, for the first half-hour Nancy had little to do other than sit back and enjoy the feeling of sun and wind on her face.

"Mmmm, this is the life," she said, rubbing sunscreen on her bare stomach. She was wearing a Day-Glo green two-piece bathing suit with black borders. It fitted her slim figure like a glove.

"I know what you mean." Bess raked her straw

blond hair into a ponytail and fastened it with a clip that matched her pink one-piece. "If only Tommy was here right now my life would be perfect. Oh, well. Pass me a chicken leg, George."

"If she can't have her boyfriend she'll settle for food," George teased.

"Let's trim the sails, folks," Emily ordered. "Nancy, the cove where you found me is over there to port. We can shoot right into it."

Nancy sat up, suddenly alert. "Let's check it out. We can work our way toward the tip of the island from there."

At Emily's command, George and Ned trimmed the sails until they were tight. Emily spun the wheel, and the *Swallow* slowly turned in the water, heeling over to one side. Spray flew from the bow as she glided into the cove.

"What are we looking for, exactly?" Ned wanted to know.

"I'm not really sure," Nancy admitted. "Overhangs, inlets—anyplace where someone could hide a boat like this."

But the shoreline in the cove was a smooth, unbroken curve, as they discovered when they sailed along its length. "I don't know, Nan," George said with a doubtful frown. "I don't think there's much in the way of overhangs or inlets in this part of the bay. It's mostly beach."

"Well, we've got to keep looking," Nancy said doggedly. "The boat had to be hidden somewhere."

Two hours later Nancy was beginning to wonder, though. They had sailed up past Montauk and around the narrow tip of Long Island, right into the open ocean, but nowhere had they seen a spot that looked suitable for hiding the *Swallow*.

"There has to be something we're overlooking," she said, thinking aloud. "Emily, try to remember what it was like where you were being held. Were there waves? What kind of noises were there? How much light came in?"

Emily squinted out at the horizon. Then her eyes opened wide. "Nancy, that's it! The light!" she cried. "There wasn't any light coming into the portholes the whole time the boat was moored!"

"Didn't you say the portholes were covered?" Ned asked, looking confused.

"Yes, they were, but one of the covers was loose. I remember seeing daylight a couple of times," Emily explained. She turned back to Nancy. "But not while we were moored. I must have been someplace dark—like one of those covered docks some people keep their boats in for winter storage. You know, with the bubblers in the water to keep ice from forming on the boats. No one ever looks inside those places until October at least."

"Brilliant," Nancy said happily. "There can't be too many of those in this area. All we have to do is find the few and check them out."

"There are only two that I know of that might be tall enough for *Swallow*'s mast," Emily said. She steadied the big chrome steering wheel. "The closest one to here is right above Montauk on the bay side. I don't know who it belongs to."

However, the first boat shed turned out to be a dead lead when they finally found it. The big door was made of corrugated steel held shut by triple padlocks. Moreover, from the way it was hung, Nancy guessed that the door slid into a track on the side of the building—and probably not without the aid of a motor. It looked *very* heavy. There was no way one person could have budged it alone.

Emily looked disappointed. "That was my best bet," she explained. "The other shed, Bob Smithson's, is down below Montauk, not too far from home. I thought we sailed farther than that."

"Don't forget that the weather was rough when you were kidnapped," Nancy pointed out. "It could have taken a long time to go a little way."

"Good point," Ned said, taking Nancy's free hand in his own. "Let's go."

"This one looks promising," George called as they approached Bob Smithson's shed later. It was in poor repair, with a wooden door that sagged on its hinges. It would be easy to break into. And there were no houses nearby. The area was deserted.

"Who's Bob Smithson?" Bess asked Emily. "Could he be the one who kidnapped you?"

Emily laughed. "I doubt it. He's about ninety

years old—I don't think he'd have the strength. He's just a man who's lived here for as long as I can remember."

An old, feeble man wouldn't be likely to check his shed very often, Nancy reflected. This was looking better and better.

Under Emily's direction, they sailed the sloop almost directly up to the shed, then veered quickly into the wind. The *Swallow*'s sails flapped in the sudden calm, and she coasted to a stop in front of the door.

"Beautiful," Nancy said appreciatively. She reached out and pushed the door. It swung inward with a creak.

"Can you bring us inside?" she asked. In answer, Emily swung the wheel around. The rudder's movement in the water gave the *Swallow* momentum to glide slowly into the shed.

Nancy jumped onto the small dock as they came alongside it. Fishing out her penlight, she peered up and down the planks.

In less than a minute she hit pay dirt. "Aha!" she said triumphantly.

Her penlight shone down on a dried mud print, made by a deck shoe—probably a man's. The mud was the same color as the dry smear she'd found on the *Swallow*'s foredeck.

"This is it," she said excitedly. "We've found the place!"

Chapter

Nine

AT LAST, a tangible piece of evidence! True, a footprint wasn't much, but it was *something*.

"Let me see!" Emily cried. She jumped lightly down to the dock and gazed at the footprint. Then she looked at Nancy. "Does that tell you anything?" she asked, sounding disappointed.

"Sure," Nancy answered. "It tells us this is where the *Swallow* was hidden. There's a matching smear on the foredeck. And it might tell us who our villain is. If we can find someone whose deck shoe matches that print, we're in business."

"But there are hundreds of people with deck shoes in the Hamptons!" Bess wailed.

"We'll start with the suspects we already

have," Nancy told her. "I guess we could ask Keith's parents if we can see his shoes."

Emily grimaced. "I doubt if they'd let us into the house," she said. "Mr. Artin never liked me much, and since Keith and I broke up, he's really been cold to me."

"All right, we'll have to come up with some plan of attack for Keith," Nancy replied. "But I'll bet Seth Cooper wears deck shoes all the time. We should be able to get a print from him."

"And Roland Lyons," Emily said instantly. "Don't leave him out."

Nancy sighed. "Okay, we'll check up on Lyons, too," she said.

"How can we compare their prints with this one? Should we take a picture?" Ned asked.

Nancy had an idea. "Is there any white paper on board?" she asked. "A napkin would be fine. And, Bess, hand me your water atomizer. I'm going to take a print of this print."

"Huh?" Bess was puzzled, but she handed Nancy a napkin and the little spritzer she used to cool herself off when she sunbathed.

"Thanks." Kneeling, Nancy laid the napkin carefully over the dried print. Then she sprayed a little water from the atomizer on the napkin and pressed the dampened paper down firmly with her palms. After a few seconds she peeled it back from the dock. A mud tracing clung to the napkin, giving Nancy a perfect replica of the print.

"Hey, neat trick!" Ned said approvingly.

"Thanks. I thought so, too," Nancy agreed, grinning. She got to her feet. "Okay, guys, let's head home. We've got work to do!"

As they sailed back to the marina, Bess said, "George and I are meeting Gary and Tommy for pizza tonight. Anyone else want to come along?"

"I've got a date with Jeff," Emily said.

"Oh, well, I guess you'll want to do something more romantic, then," Bess commented with a sly smile. She looked at Nancy and Ned. "How about you two?"

Nancy was about to agree when Ned spoke up.

"Well, I was hoping to take my girl to a nice restaurant and shower her with affection," he replied. "It's been a long time."

Nancy hadn't thought about that. She felt a guilty twinge. "Gee, that sounds fantastic," she said. "But let's make it a latish dinner. I just want to take care of one or two things first, okay?" She looked pleadingly at Ned.

Ned looked resigned. "Fine," he said. "Whenever you're ready."

It was about five-thirty when they docked. Emily went home, and Nancy, Ned, Bess, and George went back to Eloise's house.

Nancy showered, dried her hair, then quickly pulled on a short knit skirt and a loose blouse. She completed the outfit with a wide leather belt and sandals, then skipped downstairs. "How do I look?" she asked, twirling in front of Ned.

"Perfect," he told her, his eyes glowing.

"You look pretty perfect yourself," she complimented him. He was wearing gray linen slacks and a billowing white shirt that set off the slight tan he had gotten that day. His brown hair, still damp, curled around his handsome face.

"Thanks. I got a restaurant recommendation from your aunt and made a seven-thirty reservation. It was the only opening they had. Will that give us enough time to do whatever it is you want to do?" Ned asked.

"It should," Nancy assured him. She picked up the phone book and found Roland Lyons's home number. She dialed, and Lyons himself answered.

"Mr. Lyons, this is Nancy Drew," she began. "We've met once or twice. You may not remember me, but I'm a friend of Emily Terner's."

"Of course I remember you. I hear you found Emily—nice work! What can I do for you, Nancy?" Lyons's voice was friendly.

She swallowed. This was going to be embarrassing. "Well, I was wondering if you could spare the time to talk to me about where you were the night Emily disappeared."

"What?" There was a pause, and then Lyons gave a shout of laughter. "Are you saying I'm a suspect? That's the best joke I've heard in ages."

"I'd also like to show you something that I found aboard the boat," Nancy pressed on doggedly. "Would it be all right if a friend of mine and I stopped by to see you?"

Lyons was still chuckling. "Sure, come on

73

over," he said. "I'm not busy this evening. I'll think up a good alibi."

"Thanks. We'll be there in half an hour," Nancy said, and hung up. She turned to Ned. "Want to come watch me make a fool of myself?"

He grinned. "I wouldn't miss it." Then he checked his watch. "But are you sure we won't miss our dinner reservation? It's getting late."

"We'll make it," Nancy promised.

Half an hour later they pulled up in front of Lyons's house. The roadway was still under repair, Nancy noted. It must be annoying for Lyons to live with all that dust and noise.

Lyons answered the door himself. "My housekeeper's only here from nine to five," he explained. "Evenings I rough it. Can I offer you two sodas or anything?"

"Please, don't bother," Nancy said. "We don't want to take up too much of your time."

"Not at all," he said easily. "Sit down, make yourselves comfortable." He disappeared and came back a few minutes later with tall glasses of soda.

"Now, you wanted to know where I was the night Emily Terner disappeared? What fun! Let's see, when was that?"

"Last Friday," Nancy told him.

"Oh, right. As a matter of fact, I was right here, asleep in my bed." He chuckled.

Nancy began to get annoyed. Lyons was certainly getting a huge amount of amusement out of this interview. "Can you prove that?" she asked.

"Nope," Lyons said promptly. "No witnesses. But I do have a cast-iron alibi, nonetheless."

"And that is?" Nancy urged. He was obviously waiting to be asked.

Lyons leaned forward and pushed his horn-rimmed glasses up on his nose. "I can't stand boats," he told them. "Can't even get near them. Inner-ear problems. I get seasick at the drop of a hat. I wouldn't know a jib sheet from a bedsheet! You can ask anyone who knows me. I'm famous for it." He grinned at them.

It certainly *sounded* like a cast-iron alibi. If Lyons was telling the truth, he certainly couldn't have piloted the *Swallow* through rough waters at night, alone. Nancy would check up on his claim, of course, but she was sure he was telling the truth. It would be too easy to catch him if he were lying.

"So, am I still a suspect?" Lyons asked. "I hope so. Life around here has been pretty dull lately. A little melodrama is just what I need."

"At this point all I'm trying to do is eliminate some of the possibilities," Nancy responded, trying to keep the irritation out of her voice. She was almost disappointed that Lyons had such a good alibi. He would have made a great villain, with his smug smile and patronizing manner.

She put down her soda glass and stood up. "Mr. Lyons, may we look at your shoe collection?" she asked.

Lyons looked surprised for a moment. "Certainly. They're all in my closet upstairs. I'll show you." He snickered. "But I have to confess I threw the bloodstained ones away."

Ned and Nancy followed Lyons up the stairs and into his bedroom. He threw open the louvered doors of a huge closet and gestured to neat rows of shoes. "There they are. Am I guilty?"

Ned pulled the napkin out of his pocket and handed it to Nancy. She unfolded it.

It was obvious at a glance that Lyons hadn't made that muddy footprint. His feet were much too small, and, as far as Nancy could see, he didn't even have a pair of deck shoes. Well, that was that. She rose to her feet.

"Sorry to disturb your evening," she said to Lyons. "We'll be going now."

"No rush. Say, what happened to that Russian boyfriend of yours?" Lyons remarked. "I always see you two together. I thought you were inseparable."

There was an awkward silence. Nancy couldn't even look at Ned, she was so mortified. Then she gathered her wits. "Sasha's just a friend," she said. "Ned is my boyfriend."

"Oh, my mistake. Sorry," Lyons said as he showed them out. "Come back anytime," he added, chuckling again. "This was fun."

"Whew! What a jerk!" Ned said as they pulled away. "He really enjoyed that. No wonder Emily thinks he's a crook."

"Unfortunately, we're not going to pin *this*

crime on him," Nancy pointed out. "I don't see any way he could have done it."

"No, I guess not," Ned replied. He glanced at his watch and whistled. "Nor do I see any way we're going to make a seven-thirty reservation in Southhampton. It's seven now, and Southhampton's an hour's drive from here, isn't it?"

Nancy nodded, stricken. "Oh, Ned, I'm sorry. Can we do it another night?"

"Sure." Ned shrugged. "Let's get a pizza."

They drove in silence for a while. Then Ned spoke in a quiet voice.

"So—was it true, what Lyons said about Sasha and you? Are you involved with him? Is that why you've been acting so weird since I got here?"

Nancy had been waiting for that very question. Tell him everything! a little voice urged, but somehow she couldn't bring herself to do it.

"Nothing has happened between me and Sasha," she said.

"I mean, you talked about him a lot at the beginning of the summer, but then you stopped. I kind of wondered why, since you've obviously been seeing so much of him." Ned gazed intently through the windshield. His jaw was tight.

"It's not like that! I—" Nancy broke off. She felt awful. Why couldn't she explain? "I'm not involved with him," she finished lamely.

Ned was silent. "Okay," he said at last.

Dinner was double torture. They caught up with Bess and George and their boyfriends at the Pizza Shack, but Nancy soon wished they hadn't.

Sasha's name kept coming up in conversation. He had shared every adventure the girls had had over the summer, it seemed.

"Sasha sure has a nose for mystery," Gary was saying. "Remember when we thought he was involved in the theft of those plans from Jetstream? And then it turned out he actually discovered the real crook before anyone else. I guess I owe as much to him as to you, Nancy. Without the two of you, I'd probably be out of a job right now."

Nancy did her best to smile at Gary. She knew he meant well, but couldn't he see this conversation was making her uncomfortable?

"Yeah, maybe you two should consider going into business together," Tommy suggested.

"Sasha's a dancer, not a detective," Nancy said with a forced laugh.

"And besides, Nancy doesn't need a partner," Bess put in loyally. "She's got me and George and Ned—even though you complain about her cases all the time, Ned," she teased him.

Nancy suppressed a groan. Bess was trying to help, but she was only making things worse.

Poor Ned bore it all heroically. But Nancy couldn't ignore the questions and doubts she could see growing in his eyes.

Finally the party broke up. Bess and Tommy decided to go for a walk, but Gary had to work early the next morning, so George got a ride home with Nancy and Ned. Nancy tried not to be impatient—she desperately wanted to talk to

Ned, but she couldn't with George in the car. It would have to wait until they got home.

But when they pulled up to Eloise Drew's house, Nancy had a surprise waiting for her.

Eloise always left a light on over the front door, so that people could find their way up the path in the dark. In the illuminated circle, Nancy could see two people standing close together. She felt a twinge of uneasiness. One of the people was Eloise Drew. The other looked like Seth Cooper. Seth Cooper, who was rapidly becoming one of Nancy's biggest suspects.

Her uneasiness grew a moment later, as Seth drew Eloise into his arms and they shared a long, tender kiss!

Chapter

Ten

"OH, BOY," George murmured from the back-seat. "Did we pick the wrong time to arrive."

When Eloise and Seth heard the car, they broke apart. Eloise fumbled in her bag for her door key, while Seth jammed his hands into his pockets.

"I think we embarrassed them!" George exclaimed. Nancy could tell by her voice that George was trying to hold back a laugh. "I never thought I'd catch your aunt kissing! I mean, she's seen me with Gary often enough."

In spite of her anxiety, Nancy couldn't help giggling, too. It was a funny switch.

"Well, come on. Act like you didn't notice anything," she told George and Ned. The three of them walked up the path, trying to act normal. George's mouth kept twitching, though.

"Hi," Nancy called. "Just getting home?"

George snickered. "Dumb question," she whispered. Nancy glared at her.

"Well, hello," Eloise answered, sounding flustered. She finally found her key and opened the door. "Yes, we just got back from a chamber-music concert at the town hall."

"Nancy, your aunt tells me you rescued Emily Terner," Seth rumbled. "It's quite a story. Do you really believe she was kidnapped?"

Did he bring that up just for conversation's sake, or is he trying to find out what I know? Nancy wondered.

"Yes, I do," she said, moving past him into the living room. "I'm trying to find out who's guilty." She put a teasing tone in her voice. "Everyone's a suspect now—even you, Mr. Cooper. So tell me, where were *you* on Friday night?"

"Ah, that's for me to know and you to find out," he responded, but Nancy saw a glint of disquiet in his eyes.

"Oh, come on, you can tell me," she urged, smiling. If he was innocent, he'd answer openly.

Seth shrugged. "If you really want to know, I went to the movies in Montauk."

"What'd you see? *The African Queen* was playing at that great repertory theater, wasn't it? I wanted to go, but I didn't feel like driving there in the rain." Nancy made it sound as if she'd lost interest in the interrogation.

It worked. Seth nodded. "That's right. It's a great flick—you should see it sometime."

"Why are we all standing around?" Eloise asked suddenly. "Sit down and relax, everyone. Seth, can I offer you a cup of coffee?"

"No, thanks. I ought to get back to my boat," he said. He took Eloise's hand and pressed it to his lips with a flourish. "Thanks for a lovely evening."

"I should thank *you*," Eloise responded. Her cheeks pinkened slightly, but her smile was brilliant. "Why don't I walk you out to your car?"

As soon as the door clicked shut behind them, George doubled over with giggles. "They're still embarrassed," she said. "It's so cute!"

"No wonder they're embarrassed, with you around," Ned told her.

"Hey, guys, it's not that funny," Nancy said anxiously. "Seth is getting higher on my list of suspects. He lied about where he was on Friday."

"How do you know?" George asked, sobering.

"*The African Queen* wasn't playing. Last week was James Bond week," Nancy answered.

Ned frowned. "So he lied. Does that make him your kidnapper?"

"I don't know yet," Nancy said. "But I'm going to find out."

Nancy got up early on Wednesday morning and jumped into the shower. Then she went back to the big bedroom she shared with Bess and George.

They were sleeping peacefully in their twin beds. She yanked up the blinds so the sun poured in. "Rise and shine, guys," she called. "We've got a busy day!"

"Go away," George mumbled, and threw a pillow at her. Bess just moaned.

"I'll be in the kitchen making pancakes," Nancy told her friends. "Hurry down, or they'll get cold."

"Blackmailer," Bess complained to Nancy's departing back. Nancy grinned.

Soon they were all gathered around the kitchen table. Nancy stood at the griddle, outlining the day's tasks as she flipped pancakes.

"We're going to have to break up into two teams," she said, carrying a stack of cakes to the table. "Here, Ned, these are for you."

"Thanks," he said shortly. He took them without looking at her. He was still upset about the night before, Nancy realized. Well, she could talk to him as they did their errands.

"Two people will have to check out Roland Lyons's story about getting seasick. He's probably not lying, but we have to make sure," Nancy said. "I think the best way to do it is to go to his office in Montauk and get into a conversation with his secretary or something. The people he works with will probably know."

Ned looked up. "I'll go. Want to come with me, Bess?"

Bess looked taken aback. "Sure, I guess so," she said, glancing at Nancy for confirmation.

Nancy shrugged, hurt. Ned was trying to avoid her. Well, it was her own fault.

"Okay, then, George and I will check area stores to see if we can trace the flashlight and batteries," Nancy concluded.

They finished breakfast quickly, and Bess and Ned left for Montauk. Nancy and George drove into town and started on the stores.

By ten-thirty they had covered every hardware store and drugstore in town, with no luck. Nancy drove into the parking lot of one of the public beaches, then switched off the ignition and stared out the windshield at the ocean.

"We could try Southampton and Montauk," she said despondently, "but I doubt we'd have better luck. This is just a waste of time!"

"Hey, don't take it so hard," George said. "It's not vital evidence. We can still crack this case. What are you so upset about?"

Nancy sighed. "I'm just down. Didn't you notice that Ned was avoiding me this morning? And last night he went to bed without a word to me. I haven't had any time to talk to him since he got here."

"About Sasha, you mean?" George asked.

Nancy nodded, then told George about her conversation with Sasha, and about what Lyons had said, and the clumsy way she'd handled it when Ned questioned her about the relationship.

"I don't know why it's so hard to talk about it with him," she finished. "Ned is so understanding. I don't know what I'm afraid of."

"Maybe you're afraid of the choice you're going to make," George suggested. "You've been with Ned for a long time. If you're thinking of breaking up with him, that's a very big step."

"Am I prepared to break up with Ned?" Nancy wondered aloud. "The whole idea seems so unreal. Could I really leave him for Sasha?"

George shook her head. "It's a tough situation," she said sympathetically. "If you don't decide soon, though, you'll lose both of them."

"I know." Nancy started the car. "I know."

She stopped in at the florist's on the way home, to pick up flowers for the big vase in Eloise's foyer.

The florist was making up a spray of orange lilies for Keith Artin's hospital room. "Poor Keith." The florist sighed. He was a plump man with a reputation as a gossip. "Ran out of brake fluid, the police say. He should have had his car tuned more often."

"Ran out of brake fluid?" Nancy repeated. "I can't believe it. He spent all his free time working on that car, from what I heard."

The florist eyed her unkindly. "Well, he didn't check the brake fluid, I guess."

He sounded hurt that she doubted his story. Shrugging, Nancy paid for the flowers and left.

George was meeting Gary for lunch, so Nancy drove back alone. At home she found a note from Bess on the kitchen table. Lyons's story checked out, and now Bess and Ned were on the beach.

Nancy had changed into her suit and was

about to join them when the doorbell rang. She opened the front door. Her heart turned over.

Sasha stood there, a bouquet of wildflowers in his hand. "You have been avoiding me," he stated, walking into the living room. He laid the flowers on the coffee table.

"I've been busy," Nancy defended herself, although she knew he was right. She could have made time to talk if she'd been ready to face him.

"You do not wish to make a difficult decision, so you make work for yourself," Sasha said with chilling accuracy. "But I will not let you run away any longer. I need to know, Nancy."

"Wh-what?" Nancy asked. Sasha's eyes were mesmerizing—just looking at him, her thoughts got muddled and she couldn't find her tongue.

He moved swiftly forward and seized her hand. "You know I have the chance to stay here for a year. My decision would be easier if I knew your heart. I have told you that I love you. Do you love me?"

Sasha's eyes bored into Nancy's, and his hand held hers so tightly it hurt. Her heart felt as if it were about to burst from all the conflicting emotions in it. She groped for words, but all that came out was a sigh.

The sound of the deck door opening shattered the moment. Nancy turned to see who it was.

She let out an involuntary cry of distress.

It was Ned!

Chapter

Eleven

NED STOOD THERE for an instant, his face frozen in an expression of shock. Without a word, he turned and strode away. He moved so fast he was almost running.

Nancy wrenched her hand free of Sasha's. "I can't talk to you now. I have to go after him," she said tensely. "I can't let him think—"

"Think what?" Sasha pressed.

"You'd better go," Nancy said, ignoring the question, and ran after Ned. How could she have done it? How could she have hurt him so badly?

She paused at the crest of a dune and looked around. Which way had he gone? The beach was crowded, and he would be hard to spot.

"Hey, Nan!" Bess was waving to her from a

blanket. Nancy ran across the sand to her friend. "Ned went up to the house to see if you were back. Did you miss each other?" Bess asked.

"No. He found me. But he found Sasha with me," Nancy said flatly.

Bess's mouth formed a soundless *Oh*.

Nancy swallowed hard to keep the tears back. "I have to find him, Bess! I have to straighten things out!"

Bess jumped up and gave her friend a quick hug. "Good luck," she said.

Nancy managed a shaky smile. Then she hurried on down the beach, searching.

She finally found Ned about a quarter-mile from where she'd left Bess. He was sitting on the sand, gazing out at the curling breakers.

"Ned," Nancy said softly.

At the sound of her voice a muscle worked in Ned's square jaw, but he didn't look at her. "I don't want to talk to you right now," he said.

"Please let me explain." Nancy felt tears filling her eyes. He sounded so hurt!

"What is there to explain? It seems pretty clear to me," Ned replied stonily. "The only thing I don't understand is why you invited me out here in the first place."

"Because I wanted to be with you. I love you, Ned!" Nancy knelt swiftly and touched his cheek. "What I told you last night is true. Nothing's happened between Sasha and me. True, we have spent a lot of time together, and I have to admit I'm attracted to him. I should have told you this before, but I just didn't know how to say it. I'm sorry—I'm so sorry! I didn't mean to hurt you."

Ned looked at her for the first time. "What is it about him?" he asked in a raw voice. "What makes Sasha so great?"

Nancy shook her head ruefully. "I don't know if he's so great. Maybe it's just that he's different. I wish I could explain, but I really don't understand it myself. I'm confused, Ned."

"Confused? You're confused? That makes two of us," he said with a bitter laugh.

Nancy took a deep breath, then asked the question that had been burning in her heart. She dreaded what his answer might be, but still she had to know.

"So what happens now?" she said. "Do you want to break up with me?"

Ned was silent for a long moment. Then he shook his head. "I can't help being in love with you," he said simply. "No matter what. So I guess I'll just have to convince you that I'm the right guy for you."

"What?" Nancy didn't know whether to laugh or cry. "What do you mean?"

Ned shrugged, a strange, determined gleam in his eye. "What we have is special, Nancy. It's more than 'different.' And I'm not going to lose you to some summer flirtation, just because you can't see that as clearly as I can."

He stood up. "Come on, let's go back to Bess. She's probably wondering where we are."

Nancy gazed at his profile as they walked along the damp sand. She didn't quite understand what had just happened. Was Ned going to forgive and forget, just like that? She tentatively reached out and took his hand.

He didn't squeeze it warmly, the way he usually did, but he didn't reject it, either. It was going to take time, Nancy realized. But if she kept trying, maybe she could win his trust again.

Tommy, Jeff, and Emily had joined Bess on her beach blanket. "Hey, I'm working the afternoon shift. Do you two want to come water-skiing?" Tommy called as Nancy and Ned walked up.

"Definitely," Ned agreed.

Bess looked anxiously at Nancy. "Is everything okay?" she mouthed. Nancy shrugged. She couldn't tell—maybe it was, with Ned. But there was still Sasha to deal with.

"Nancy, the police called. They found the *Swallow*'s dinghy this morning," Emily said. "It washed ashore near Smithson's shed. No fingerprints, of course. They're still complaining that they have no solid leads."

Nancy frowned, her mind back on the case. "Did you tell them about the footprint?" she asked.

"First thing when I got home yesterday," Emily told her. "They checked it out and called back, saying it could have been made anytime, and that even if it is the kidnapper's print, millions of men have size-ten deck shoes. At least they found out what size it was," she added. "Maybe that'll help us."

Tommy stood up, brushing sand from the seat of his multicolored trunks. "Let's head over to the bay," he suggested. "My shift starts soon."

Nancy helped Bess fold up the blanket and they went out to the street, where Tommy and Jeff's jeep was parked. As they walked, Nancy dropped slightly behind the group. She beckoned to Emily and Tommy.

"What's up?" Tommy asked, falling into step beside Nancy. Emily walked on her other side.

"I need your advice," Nancy told him. "You probably know more about Seth Cooper than I do." She described how Seth had lied about where he was on Friday night. "I know he didn't go to the movies," she finished. "The question is, what *was* he doing? Is he our kidnapper?"

Tommy looked troubled. "Now that you mention it, I wonder if he could be. I stopped by his boat, *Twice Shy,* early Saturday morning—around seven. I wanted to tell him the regatta had been postponed, but he wasn't there. I was surprised, but I didn't really think about it."

Nancy lifted her eyebrows. So Seth was unaccounted for during the entire period of time when the kidnapper must have been grabbing Emily and stowing her in Smithson's shed. "He's looking likelier," she said.

"But why, Nancy?" Emily broke in. "He has no motive. I just can't believe winning a race could mean that much to someone."

"Maybe there's some other reason we don't know about yet," Nancy theorized. "Or maybe he's a little crazy. All I know is, he had both ability and opportunity. I've got to check him out."

They reached the jeep, and all six of them piled in. Jeff squeezed behind the wheel, and they were off.

"Hey—isn't that Sasha?" Tommy exclaimed as they passed a walking figure. "What's he doing in this neighborhood? He must have gone by your house looking for you, Nancy. Pull over, Jeff. Hey, Sasha, want to come water-skiing?"

Mortified, Nancy put out her hand to stop him, but it was too late. Sasha jogged over to the jeep. He looked cheerful and unconcerned, as if nothing had happened between him and Nancy just a short while ago.

"Is there room?" he asked.

"Sure," Ned put in heartily. Nancy stared at him in shock as he opened the door. "Hi, I'm Ned Nickerson. Squeeze in—we can fit one more."

Nancy was flabbergasted. Even the unflappable Sasha looked momentarily taken aback, but then he shrugged and climbed in. "I suppose these shorts will do as trunks" was all he said.

What's going on? Nancy wondered as the jeep

started moving again. She gave Ned a hard look, but he just smiled blandly at her.

Soon they arrived at the ski-rental shop where Tommy worked. He worked there every summer, and his boss let him use the boats and equipment for free every now and then.

"Who wants to go first?" Tommy asked. "Ned, you're the stranger in town—why don't you?"

"Thanks. I will," Ned replied. "I see you've got two towropes. I can share the skis, if anyone else knows how to single-ski. Sasha, want to try your luck with me?"

Nancy and Bess exchanged horrified glances. What was Ned up to?

"Why not?" Sasha agreed. He smiled slowly at Ned. "Maybe I can show you a few new tricks."

"But Sasha's just a beginner!" Bess whispered to Nancy. "What does he think he's doing?"

"Hey, it sounds like fun. Can I try after Sasha?" Emily put in. Her eyes were sparkling with eagerness.

Nancy stepped forward quickly. "I don't think it's a good idea," she said. "It sounds danger-ous."

"Oh, don't be a stick-in-the-mud," Emily teased. "What could happen?"

"I guess it's fine, as long as you both know what you're doing," Tommy said.

So Nancy was overruled, and Ned and Sasha went out together. Bess and Nancy elected to stay ashore with Emily and Jeff.

"I can't believe Ned is doing this. And I can't believe Sasha is going along with it!" Nancy exclaimed to Bess when they were alone. Emily and Jeff were sitting by themselves, talking quietly. Nancy looked out at the skiers. They were crossing each other's wakes, skipping over the waves and making sharp, dangerous turns.

Bess sat down on the sun-warmed dock. "Ned is being awfully competitive, isn't he?" she said. "I never knew he was like that."

"He's not, usually," Nancy replied. "I think he's trying to prove something. But this is stupid."

Both Ned and Sasha were excellent athletes in different ways. Sasha's skiing was smooth and graceful, with a fluid style that made it look effortless. Ned moved with raw power, cutting through the waves as though they didn't exist.

Then, as the girls watched, Tommy swung into a sharp curve. Sasha seemed to be trying to keep his balance. One hand flew up in the air. Then he toppled over, still holding the towrope.

"He's down," Bess said. "Why doesn't he let go of the rope?"

Nancy leapt up, her heart hammering. "He can't!" she cried. "His hand must be caught! Oh, doesn't Tommy see what's happening?"

But the boat kept going at top speed. And behind it, Sasha was being dragged through the waves headfirst. If he didn't break free, he'd drown!

Chapter

Twelve

FRANTIC, NANCY WAVED HER ARMS over her head to signal Tommy. "Stop the boat!" she screamed.

Bess clutched Nancy's arm. "Look!" she cried. "Ned saw what happened. He's going to save him."

Nancy felt her breath catch in her throat. Ned was cutting right across the wake of the powerboat, his ski slicing through the water. In an instant he was at Sasha's side. The boat still surged through the water at full speed as Ned reached down and grabbed the taut tow-rope.

"Oh, I can't watch," Bess said, turning away. "They're both going to be killed!"

But she was wrong. Ned must have managed to untangle Sasha's rope, because suddenly the line went slack. Then Ned let go of his own towrope and sank down into the water. Nancy could see that he was holding Sasha's head above the waves with one hand and treading water with the other.

Tommy had apparently realized something was wrong. The powerboat slowed, then cut back to the two bobbing heads in a tight arc. Tommy cut the engine and leaned over the side to haul Ned and Sasha into the boat. They were safe!

Nancy sagged against Bess, limp with relief. "It's okay," she told her friend. "They're all right."

Tommy brought the boat back to the dock immediately. He looked pale and shaken as he climbed out of the pilot's seat. Bess ran to his side and hugged him. "I should have seen what was happening," he kept saying. "I should have seen."

Ned and Jeff helped Sasha onto the dock. Then Ned turned to Tommy. "It's not your fault," he said. "The whole thing happened in less than a minute. Don't be so hard on yourself."

"Ned," Sasha began, then stopped short as a fit of coughing overtook him. He leaned against a post. When it was over he tried again.

"You saved my life," he said hoarsely. "Thank you."

"I didn't save your life," Ned said, sounding almost angry. "Even if I hadn't seen you fall, Tommy would've figured it out any second."

Sasha gazed at him for a moment. "Nevertheless, I thank you," he said at last.

Ned scowled. "For what it's worth, you're welcome." He turned away and reached for a towel.

Everyone was silent and subdued on the ride home. They dropped Sasha off at his house first, and Emily and Jeff helped him inside. Then they drove to Eloise Drew's house.

"I'm having dinner with the Grays," Bess said, looking apologetically at Nancy. "Are you going to be okay without me?" she whispered.

"I'll be fine. Have fun," Nancy told her, squeezing her arm. "See you later."

As soon as they got inside, Ned headed for the stairs. "I'm going to take a shower," he called over his shoulder. "And then I might take a nap. I'm beat."

"Ned, are you all right?" Nancy asked.

He didn't stop. "I'm fine," he said curtly. "Just tired. See you in a bit."

Nancy sat down on the cream-colored sofa and gazed thoughtfully at the empty fireplace. One thing was obvious: whatever was happening with her and Ned and Sasha wasn't over yet.

George came in at about six, looking radiant. "Gary took the afternoon off, and we walked on the beach and talked," she said. "Oh, Nancy, he's so wonderful! I've never met anyone like him."

Nancy smiled at her friend's happiness.

"Hey, where is everyone?" George asked.

"I'm here," came a new voice, and Eloise Drew swept in with an armful of packages. "But only for a second. Seth and I have a reservation at Le Jardin in Southampton. I bought a new dress, and I've got to change." She gave a girlish giggle.

Nancy and George looked at each other as Eloise hurried up the stairs. "A new dress?" George echoed. "This sounds serious."

"It also sounds like my chance to search Seth's boat," Nancy said, thinking aloud.

George made a face. "And *that* sounds risky. For more than one reason."

"I have to do it. He's a suspect," Nancy said. "I just hope Aunt Eloise doesn't find out."

Ned came downstairs rubbing his eyes. He looked a bit more cheerful, Nancy was glad to see.

"Good morning, Mr. Nickerson," George said with a laugh. "Did you sleep well?"

Ned grinned. "Like a baby."

Nancy told him her plan to search Seth's boat. "Do you want to come along?" she asked diffidently. She wasn't sure he would.

"I'm there," he answered immediately, much to her relief. "I can keep an eye out in case he comes back early."

"Great! Now all we have to do is wait until dark," Nancy said.

Time flew by while they cooked and ate dinner. They finished cleaning up just before nine, and Nancy and Ned went up to change into dark clothing. George had decided to stay at home.

"I feel stupid in all this black," Ned complained as they walked to the car. "It's summer, and we're at the beach! Everyone who sees us is going to think we're burglars."

"We are, in a way," Nancy reminded him. "And anyway, the whole idea of dressing like this is so people *won't* see us."

"Yeah, I guess so," Ned agreed.

A thick fog was creeping in from the bay, Nancy noted with satisfaction. The weather would give them good cover.

They parked near the marina and then crept through the parking lot. Ms. Hanks was still in her office. Nancy could see her through the window, sitting at her desk.

There were two or three people puttering around at their boats. Nancy and Ned waited in the shadows next to the equipment storage shed until they had all gone. Then they hurried down the dock to Seth's boat, the *Twice Shy*.

"I'm going in. Wait by that post over there, okay?" Nancy told Ned in a low voice. "Do you think you'll recognize Seth if you see him?"

Ned nodded. "If I see him, I'll whistle," he promised.

"Good." Nancy would have kissed him, but she still felt unsure of how he would react. So instead she just smiled at him. Then she climbed into the cockpit of the *Twice Shy*.

It was a slightly bigger boat than the *Swallow*, but with the same clean lines and long, sharp prow. Seth had obviously bought it with the intention of racing it. Nancy looked around admiringly. He certainly kept it spotlessly clean.

The fog was getting thicker by the minute. As Nancy reached for the hatch to the cabin, a horn hooted a mournful five-second blast.

The hatch was locked, but Nancy had brought a stiff piece of wire with her. In a jiffy she picked the lock and stepped inside the cabin.

A fair amount of light came in from a lamp mounted on a post right outside the *Twice Shy*'s slip. Nancy could see that the cabin was as neat as the cockpit. Seth's bunk was made up army-style, his shoes lined up in rows by the foot.

Pulling out the napkin with the muddy print, Nancy knelt by a pair of deck shoes. She picked one up and held it to the print.

It matched exactly!

Nancy's heart sank. Seth seemed nice enough, but he was looking guiltier and guiltier. How would her aunt take it if he turned out to be the kidnapper?

She pushed the worry aside and tucked the shoe inside her dark blue windbreaker. It was material evidence. She had what she'd come for.

While I'm here, I might as well look for more clues, she thought. Outside, the foghorn hooted again. Nancy scanned the cabin.

A small built-in desk by the galley looked promising. It had two drawers, one with a lock.

The unlocked drawer proved to hold nothing but some stationery and a few stray pens. Nancy closed it and turned to the other.

It took but a moment's work to pick the lock, and the minute she opened the drawer, Nancy's eyes widened.

On top of a stack of papers lay a framed photo. Nancy pulled out her penlight and clicked it on so that she could see the details clearly.

The photo looked recent. It showed a smiling, tanned Seth Cooper aboard the *Twice Shy*. He had his arm around a beautiful red-haired woman. And the wedding ring on his finger showed up clearly against her silk-clad shoulder.

Seth Cooper was a married man!

"That *rat!*" Nancy fumed. She slammed the photo down on the desktop. "I'll bet a million dollars he never told Aunt Eloise about his wife!"

Poor Eloise. She was dating a two-timer who was quite possibly a kidnapper as well.

Nancy looked back in the drawer. There was a pile of typewritten pages that looked as if they had been shoved in there in haste. It was the only untidy thing Nancy had seen on the boat so far.

The foghorn let out another long blast. Pulling the sheaf of pages out, Nancy squinted at the tiny type. It looked like a legal document of some kind. Hmm, she thought. This could be worthwhile.

A cool breeze tickled the back of her neck. Suddenly alert, Nancy froze.

Even so, the deep, booming voice caught her by surprise. "Nancy Drew! What are you doing snooping around my cabin?"

Seth Cooper was back!

Chapter

Thirteen

Nancy's mind raced. Seth was back early.
Either Ned hadn't seen him—or, more likely, the
foghorn had drowned out Ned's whistle.

Slowly Nancy turned around. Act cool, take
him off guard, she told herself. Assuming that
Ned was on the alert outside, she could afford to
go on the offensive. If Seth tried anything violent,
Ned would be there to help.

"I'll explain what I'm doing in your cabin, Mr.
Cooper, if you'll explain where you *really* were
last Friday night, or why your footprint was on
the dock in Bob Smithson's boat shed," she said
in a brisk tone.

"What?" Seth took a step backward. He looked

utterly confused. Nancy felt a moment of uncertainty. Could he be that good an actor?

She realized she'd gone too far to back down now, though. She stood up, brandishing the sheaf of documents. "And while we're at it, can you tell me what's in these very suspicious-looking legal documents? Or why you never bothered to tell my aunt that you're married?"

Seth's face darkened with anger. "What are you—oh!" And then, to Nancy's immense surprise, he threw back his head and let out a great roar of laughter!

When his amusement finally subsided, he looked at Nancy and wiped his streaming eyes. "I'm sorry," he said weakly, "but I think we've misunderstood each other for too long, Nancy. We need to talk. Come out on deck and sit. It's less stuffy outside."

With a sinking feeling in her stomach, Nancy followed him outside and sat on one of the cushioned cockpit seats. She suspected she'd just made a fool of herself again.

Spotting Ned, she beckoned to him. He came over, with a questioning glance at Seth.

"I whistled, but the foghorn drowned me out," he told Nancy in an undertone.

"So you're the lookout man," Seth said. "Have a seat. I'm about to clear myself of Emily's kidnapping—you might as well hear, too."

Nancy took Ned's hand and pulled him down on the seat beside her.

"Is this big goof number two?" he murmured.

Nancy nodded ruefully.

Seth sat opposite them and leaned forward, his elbows resting on his knees. "Let's start with where I was Friday night, and why I lied," he said. "And by the way, Nancy, I checked the movie listings when I got home last night and saw how you tripped me up. That was good."

Nancy didn't know quite how to react. "Thanks, I guess," she replied.

"Anyway," Seth went on, "I was in New York City on Friday night. Because the weather was so bad, I stayed the night in a hotel. I didn't get back here until eight Saturday morning. I came back early for the regatta."

That must have been why he was so annoyed that it had been postponed, Nancy thought. If he was telling the truth, he'd probably gotten up at five in the morning to get back for it.

"Why were you in the city?" she asked.

"I was having dinner with my lawyer," Seth responded. "My *divorce* lawyer."

"Oh," Nancy murmured as the truth hit her.

"That's right." Seth clasped his head in his hands for a moment, raking his fingers through his iron-gray hair. "The woman in that photograph is—was—my wife. As of this morning, when I received the official divorce papers, she is my ex-wife."

"But why did you lie about where you were?" Nancy asked. "I don't see the point."

Seth scowled. "My divorce is nobody's business but my own. As it happens, I ran into Claudia—that's my ex-wife—in the city later that evening. There was an unpleasant scene, and it left me with a bad taste in my mouth. I didn't feel like talking about the evening, especially not with your aunt Eloise around."

"I guess there are plenty of witnesses to back up your story," Ned said. Seth nodded.

"Does my aunt know about your wife, and the divorce, and everything?" Nancy asked. She might as well get that straight.

"Of course she does," Seth said, sounding indignant. "Not in great detail, but I did tell her what my status was—probably within the first half-hour after we met. After all, it's one of the biggest parts of my life at the moment. I don't like to harp on it, but I don't make a secret of it, either."

Nancy had one last question. She showed Seth the napkin with the print.

"Can you explain how this footprint, which matches the pattern and size of your deck shoe, got to be in a boat shed near Montauk? The same boat shed where we think Emily was held captive?"

Seth examined the napkin carefully, then sat back and shrugged. "You've got me there. But may I point out that I wear a size-ten shoe, which is not an uncommon size, and that I bought my deck shoes in the shoe store right here in town.

There are probably dozens of men in this area with the same kind of shoes, walking around making prints just like mine."

Nancy nodded. She'd known all along the shoeprint wouldn't be conclusive evidence. Seth had seemed guilty for other reasons as well, but his story had the ring of truth.

She sighed. "Mr. Cooper, I feel awful. I broke into your boat, invaded your privacy, and accused you of a crime you couldn't have committed. I hope you'll accept my apology."

"Well spoken," Seth said, holding out his hand. "I do accept. And I hope we can be friends, Nancy, because if I have anything to say about it, I'm going to be seeing a lot more of your aunt."

"I'll put in a good word for you." Nancy grinned, feeling a lot better. "I'll tell her how neat and tidy you are. Good night, Mr. Cooper." Seth's booming laugh followed Nancy and Ned as they walked up the dock.

Ms. Hanks was getting ready to lock the big gates. "Wait, let us out first, please!" Nancy called.

Ms. Hanks looked at them in astonishment. "I never saw you two come in," she said. "Well, at any rate, good night. I'm off to bed. It's nearly eleven o'clock."

As they got into the car, Nancy yawned. She suddenly realized what a long day it had been. "I'm exhausted," she murmured. "It's a good thing you're driving, Ned. I'd probably fall asleep at the wheel."

"We'll be home in five minutes. Then you can fall asleep in your own bed," Ned promised.

"Mmmm." It was Bess's night for the futon, Nancy thought with relief. After a day like today, she could use a soft bed. Her love life was in chaos, and her investigation was at a dead end. She was definitely feeling sorry for herself.

When Nancy came down to breakfast the next morning, she found Bess, George, Ned, and Eloise already gathered at the kitchen table. Eloise looked at her as she walked into the room.

"Ned told us what you two did last night," she said. "If only you had asked me about Seth."

Nancy poured herself a glass of juice. "I'm really sorry," she replied contritely. "I was afraid you'd be upset that I even suspected him. But I should have talked to you."

"Well, I hope you'll know better the next time," Eloise replied. "But I suppose it all ended well enough. I take it Seth is no longer on your list of suspects?"

"That's right," Nancy agreed.

"Where does that leave you?" her aunt asked.

Nancy had thought about that while she took her morning shower. "I've got to go back to our first suspect—Keith Artin," she said. "I stopped pursuing him when I heard he was in the hospital because I didn't see how I could find out anything from him."

"Well, what can you do?" Bess asked. "I don't think he's regained consciousness yet."

"I can talk to his parents and his friends," Nancy answered. "And it might be a good idea to try to get a look at his car. He had the accident the same day I found Emily. If he *is* involved, maybe there'll be some clues in the car."

"Smart girl," George said. "Need any help?"

"No, but I wouldn't mind company." Nancy smiled at Bess and Ned. "Does either of you feel like coming along?"

"Let's all go," Bess suggested. "And then we can go to the beach. Emily wants to organize a picnic and a volleyball game this afternoon."

It was settled. After breakfast the four friends drove over to Keith Artin's house. However, when Nancy rang the doorbell of the opulent-looking stucco building, no one answered. No one seemed to be at home.

Next they headed for the repair shop right outside of town. Keith's car had been towed there after the accident. Nancy had noticed it once or twice as she drove by. The once-jaunty red sports car was in sad shape, its sleek body battered and its windshield smashed.

The mechanic at the shop didn't mind them poking around at all. "If you see anything you like, let me know," he called after them. "A lot of these babies are for sale."

Nancy peered through the spiderweb of cracks on the windshield, but the interior of Keith's car appeared to be empty.

"Let's try the trunk," she suggested. Opening

the door, she found the trunk release on the dashboard and pulled it.

"This trunk's going to be hard to open," Ned cautioned. "It's pretty badly dented."

He hooked his fingers under it and pulled up, grunting with the effort. The lid moved about an inch, then stuck.

Nancy got on one side of Ned, and George got on the other. On the count of three, they heaved together. The lid rose with a reluctant creak.

Nancy peered inside. A yellow slicker and a pair of muddy deck shoes lay on the floor. And there was something else—a faint, sickly-sweet odor. She reached in and felt around for a second, then pulled out a scrap of gauze. The smell of chloroform still clung faintly to it.

"Jackpot," she said with quiet elation. She took out the napkin with the shoeprint and compared it to one of the shoes in the trunk. It fitted. More proof.

Nancy looked around at her friends. "We've got him," she announced. "Keith Artin is our culprit!"

Chapter

Fourteen

Hurray!" Bess cheered. "Case closed. Do we go to the police now?"

Nancy nodded. "I guess we do."

After a brief silence George spoke up. "I don't know why this doesn't seem complete to me. I mean, this is solid evidence, isn't it? Keith did threaten Emily. I heard him," she said. But there was a hesitant note in her voice.

"It seems weird to be pinning a crime on a guy who's lying in a hospital bed, unconscious," Ned put in. "He can't defend himself."

Slowly Nancy lowered the lid of the trunk. "Let's face it, none of us likes this solution," she said. "I still think that if Keith were trying to get revenge on Emily, he wouldn't do it this way. But the evidence says he did do it."

"So?" Bess prompted.

"So maybe there's more to the story. Maybe there's something we don't know about. If so, I'd rather find out what it is before I go to the police with this evidence."

Bess sighed with relief. "I never thought I'd say this, but I'm glad you're not giving up, Nan. Even if he is a jerk, I can't believe anyone as cute as Keith could be a kidnapper."

They all laughed. "Bess, you're a lunatic," Nancy told her friend affectionately. "Come on, I'll drop you guys at home. Take my stuff to the beach, will you? I'm going to the hardware store to see if Keith's boss can tell me anything."

When they got back to the house, Ned opted to go to the beach with Bess and George. Nancy tapped her fingers worriedly on the steering wheel as she drove away.

She still couldn't tell whether or not Ned had forgiven her. He was acting friendly enough, but he wasn't being affectionate. Nancy felt as if there was still a barrier between them. Even though she didn't like it, she knew she couldn't break it down. Ned would have to do that—when he was ready.

She parked in front of the hardware store and went in. It was humming with activity. Old Mr. Engel, the proprietor, hurried from customer to customer, and Nancy had to wait quite a while before there was a lull to speak to him.

When the store finally emptied out a bit, she approached the grizzled owner. He was bending over several piles of nails on the counter, sorting them out.

"Wouldn't you know it, the shelf collapsed this morning," he complained, "and all my nails got mixed together. Can I help you, young lady?"

Nancy introduced herself. "It looks awfully busy in here," she added. "I guess you really miss having Keith Artin around to help you."

Mr. Engel snorted angrily. "Don't talk to me about that good-for-nothing," he grumbled. "I hear he spoke a few words last night. I'm glad to know he's getting better, but I wouldn't hire him back if he got down on his knees and begged me!"

Keith had come out of his coma? Nancy's eyes widened in surprise. "I hadn't heard," she said.

"Heard what? That that young Judas quit on me, without so much as a day's notice?" Mr. Engel was working himself into a towering rage. Slightly alarmed, Nancy took a step backward.

"No, I meant I hadn't heard that he was getting better," she replied. "But I didn't know he quit, either."

Mr. Engel swept a pile of tenpenny nails into an empty box and labeled it. "Monday morning he calls and tells me he won't be in anymore," he said, jabbing his pen at Nancy for emphasis. "Didn't have the nerve to come in and say it to my face. If he doesn't like honest hard work, then good riddance to him!"

Monday morning? Nancy was suddenly alert.

That must have been right after Keith set Emily adrift in the *Swallow*. He set her adrift, rowed ashore, and then phoned in to quit his job. What was the connection?

"Did Keith say why he was quitting?" she asked Mr. Engel.

He shook his head. "Just said he didn't need it. What reasons could he give? It's a good job."

The door opened to admit another customer. Mr. Engel gave Nancy a harried look. "Excuse me. I've got customers to attend to. Now, was there something you wanted to buy?"

Nancy was afraid he'd get upset if she said no, so she bought some light bulbs. Pondering what she'd learned, she drove back to the beach.

When she got there, Emily's picnic was in full swing. There was quite a crowd. Emily, Bess, George, and Ned were there, of course, and Nancy spotted some other people she knew, too. Gary had come by on his lunch break and was helping Jeff and Tommy set up a volleyball net.

Nancy's stomach turned over when she saw Sasha down by the water's edge, but she was relieved to see that his Soviet dance partner, Marina, was with him. Maybe she'd keep him busy. Nancy didn't feel like resuming their talk right then.

Unlike Sasha, Marina didn't often mix with nondancers. In fact, she didn't seem to do much besides practice, but she was a nice girl, and she and Sasha were good friends.

She was also quite a beauty, with thick dark

113

hair and a lithe, slender figure. Nancy wondered why Marina and Sasha had never become an item, but they didn't seem interested in each other that way.

"Hi," Emily called. She beckoned Nancy over. "Join the party. Did you see that Marina's here? I couldn't believe it when I saw her. Oh, and I should warn you—she looked very interested when I introduced her to your boyfriend, Ned."

"Did she?" Nancy laughed. "He probably didn't even notice. He has no idea how cute he is."

She turned to look for Ned, but he wasn't where he had been a moment ago. Nancy scanned the beach—and blinked in surprise. Ned was down by the water, with Sasha and Marina!

They looked like they were having a great time, too. Sasha scooped up some water and splashed Marina, and in a few seconds the three of them were having a tremendous splash-fest.

"Look at that." Emily sounded amazed. "I've never seen Marina actually have fun before. I don't know, Nancy. If I were you I'd keep an eye on Ned. I think she's after him."

"Ned can take care of himself," Nancy said with a smile. But privately she was a little bothered. She watched Ned make a playful grab for Marina's arm. He did seem to be responding to the Soviet girl rather enthusiastically, didn't he?

Shrugging off her annoyance, Nancy went over

to Bess and George. They were lying on a blanket, baking themselves in the sun.

Nancy dropped down on the blanket. "Hi," she said, peeling off her shorts and T-shirt. She had her green two-piece on underneath. "Bess, can we persuade you to go swimming today?"

"Maybe." Bess looked up at the waves. "It does look tempting," she conceded. "Hey, Ned and Sasha are getting to be buddies, aren't they? What's going on? And who's that girl with Sasha?"

"You mean Marina?" Nancy asked.

"No—I know Marina. I mean that tall blond girl. The one who's flirting with Sasha."

Nancy looked where Bess was pointing. A leggy girl with shining ash-blond hair had joined Ned, Marina, and Sasha at the water's edge. They were all sitting on the sand now, talking. And the blond girl was definitely flirting with Sasha, reaching out to tap his knee playfully, tossing her hair so that it glistened in the sunlight.

Nancy's eyes narrowed. She recognized the girl from a couple of parties, but she didn't know her name. Sasha looked as if he was enjoying her attention, though.

"I can't believe Sasha's responding to that," Nancy muttered, annoyed.

Suddenly Bess gasped. "Don't look now," she said, "but Marina's all over Ned!"

Nancy's head snapped around. It was true! Marina was kneeling behind Ned, running her hands up and down his muscular back.

"Oh, she's just putting sunscreen on his back," Bess said after a minute. "Sorry, false alarm."

"False alarm? She's after him! Of all the nerve," Nancy fumed. "Doesn't she know it's rude to flirt with other people's boyfriends? And Ned! He's grinning like an idiot." Steaming, she turned around so that her back was to Ned's group. "I don't want to watch this."

"Fine," Bess said. "I'll watch for you." Then her eyes widened again. "You should see what that blond girl is doing to Sasha! I swear, she's draped around his neck like a feather boa!"

"Is Marina copying her?" Nancy asked sourly.

"No." Bess craned her neck, then turned to Nancy. "She's talking to Ned."

"Hmm. Talking, huh?" Nancy muttered. "How come she never seemed interested in talking to any of *us?* I can imagine what she's saying: 'I'm just a lonely ballerina. I have no friends here. It would be so nice if a handsome American boy would show me around. . . .'"

Nancy trailed off, then realized Bess and George were staring at her.

"Hey, they're just talking," Bess said. "They're not eloping or anything. Calm down."

Nancy took a deep breath. "You're right, I'm getting carried away. It's just that Marina's so beautiful! But I guess Ned's old enough to make his own choices." Forcing herself to relax, Nancy stretched out on the blanket and closed her eyes. "Just keep me posted, okay?"

George poked her. "Hey, I think you just made

a choice yourself," she said softly. "I think Ned is the guy you really love."

"What are you talking about?" Nancy opened one eye and squinted at George.

"Well, when that girl was flirting with Sasha, you got a little jealous. But when Marina started doing the same thing to Ned, it bothered you more. And once you started worrying about Ned, it didn't faze you that someone was all over Sasha. All you cared about was Ned."

Nancy sat up. "You're right," she said slowly. "You know what? I think I've been reaching that conclusion myself over the past few days."

She thought about the two boys. It was beginning to come clear to her.

Sasha had come into Nancy's life in an exciting way, and his attention had been immensely flattering. He admired her. He was handsome, charming, and on his way to being famous, and yet he'd admired plain old Nancy Drew.

Sasha was very, very different from Nancy. That difference made him highly attractive, in a strange way.

But Ned was like a part of her. He knew her better than anyone else. They'd been together for a long time, and she trusted him. It hurt when they weren't in tune with each other. Losing Ned would be like cutting her own heart in two.

No one else, she realized now, not even Sasha, had ever made her feel the same tingling excitement that she felt when Ned held her in his arms and kissed her.

"Hey, we're out of soda." Emily stood over the girls' blanket, blocking the sun. "Nancy, would you mind going into town to get some more?"

"Huh? Oh, sure." Nancy was glad for the errand. It would give her time to get her thoughts in order. Then she'd have to come up with a way to show Ned that she really did love him.

Bess and George went with Nancy to help her carry. The only parking place they found was in front of the hardware store.

Nancy glanced idly in the window and saw Roland Lyons at the counter. She remembered seeing him there the past Friday, before Emily disappeared. He'd been talking to Keith.

Something clicked in Nancy's mind.

She stopped short, her mind racing. Lyons and Keith. Keith and Lyons. Pinkish dried mud on Keith's shoes—red mud in front of Lyons's house. Lyons had probably overheard Emily say in the diner that she was digging into his past. Later that same day Emily had vanished.

Gradually the pieces fell into place, and Nancy began to guess what *really* happened the night Emily disappeared.

Chapter

Fifteen

WHAT'S THE MATTER, NAN?" Bess asked.

"Where's the nearest pay phone?" Nancy asked, barely hearing Bess's question.

"There's one in front of the grocery store," George told her. "What's going on?"

"I just had an idea. What if Emily was right about Roland Lyons?" Nancy said over her shoulder as she hurried to the phone.

"What about him?" George called, but Nancy was already dialing a long-distance number.

"River Heights *Morning Record,*" a voice on the other end of the line answered.

Her heart pounding with excitement, Nancy asked for Ann Granger. Ann was a reporter whom Nancy had once helped out of a tight spot.

Since then, the two had remained in touch, and Ann often used her network of sources to help Nancy.

Unfortunately, Ann was out of the office on an assignment. She wasn't expected back until late afternoon. Nancy left a message, asking Ann to call her at Eloise Drew's house.

The girls went into the grocery store. "So what's going on?" Bess asked again.

"Okay, here it is," Nancy replied, keeping her voice low. "Remember last Friday, when we had lunch with Emily, she told us she was digging up dirt on Lyons? And remember that he was there?"

"Yes, but so what? She didn't find out anything," George pointed out.

"True, but Lyons didn't hear that. Emily started whispering when she told us she hadn't had any luck. Before that—before she noticed him—she was speaking in a normal voice." She paused while the cashier rang up the six two-liter bottles of soda and put them in bags.

After the girls were back in the car, Nancy resumed, "Now, let's suppose for a second that Lyons *does* have something to hide. Something that would jeopardize his condo deal if the board knew about it. What would he do?"

"Well, he didn't kidnap Emily," Bess said. "We know Keith did that. We've got proof."

"Yes, but why couldn't Keith have worked *with* Lyons?" Nancy asked. "He wanted revenge for being dumped. Lyons wanted to keep his million-dollar deal safe." Nancy's excitement grew as she saw how neatly it all fitted together. "Keith and Emily had a public fight—maybe Lyons heard about it and saw an opportunity to use Keith to do his dirty work. All Keith had to do was get Emily out of the way until the contract was signed. Maybe Lyons promised Keith a share in the condo deal," Nancy added, thinking about how Keith had quit his job. "And Keith would also have the pleasure of helping to ruin Emily's favorite beach."

"Wow!" Bess exclaimed. "Do you really think that could have happened?"

"How are you going to prove it?" George asked. "You don't have any evidence linking Lyons to the crime."

"I do have evidence that links Keith and Lyons—the mud on Keith's shoes comes from right outside Lyons's house—but that's not proof of the crime. I'm working on it. I'm going to ask Ann Granger to find out about Lyons's business in California," Nancy said. She frowned thoughtfully. "But you're right, I do need proof before I can go to the police."

"You could call Roland Lyons's old partner," Bess suggested. "Maybe he knows something."

Nancy shook her head. "Even if he does, he wouldn't talk to Emily. I doubt he'd feel any different about talking to me. Maybe he has something to hide, too. Also, I'd hate to risk the old partner tipping off Lyons about what I'm doing. No, I'll have to wait and talk to Ann this afternoon." They arrived at the beach and delivered the soda to Emily, and then Bess and George ran over to the volleyball game that was now in progress.

Nancy had decided not to tell Emily anything until she had more information. The girl was too personally involved—she might not be able to keep quiet about Nancy's theory.

"Welcome back," Emily said. "I think you'd better check up on Ned. Marina's after him."

Nancy looked around for Ned. She finally spotted him some distance down the beach. Her eyes opened wide in astonishment.

Ned was buried in sand up to his chest. Marina and Sasha were heaping more on him, laughing as they worked. The blond girl had vanished. But the three of them—Ned, Sasha, and Marina—seemed to be having the best time in the world.

Nancy put her hands on her hips. "Something very weird is going on," she told Emily. Ned flirting with Marina was one thing, but Ned and Sasha acting like long-lost brothers was something else. And neither of them had paid any attention to *her* all day. What were they up to?

"I think they're ganging up on you," Emily said with a shrewd glance at Nancy.

Could Emily be right? Nancy wondered, shocked. Were Ned and Sasha teaming up to tell her they were tired of waiting for her to make up her mind? It made sense, in a way.

At that moment Ned caught sight of her. He broke one hand free from his sandy grave and waved at her. Marina stuffed his hand back in the sand. Then she brushed his hair back from his forehead, her hand lingering to caress his face.

Nancy gasped and turned away. Whatever else was going on, Emily was definitely right about Marina. "I can't believe this," she said. "How am I going to get him away from her?"

Emily shrugged. "Don't try," she advised. "Ned is just giving you a taste of your own medicine. Grit your teeth and ignore it."

So, for the rest of the picnic, Nancy had to seethe in silence. If Ned wanted to play games, she could certainly play along with him. But it was hard to watch him with Marina, just the same.

She took some of her edginess out in a hard-hitting game of volleyball and a long swim with George. But Nancy was glad when the party finally broke up at about four-thirty.

Ned came up as she was stuffing her things into her beach bag. "Mind if I borrow the car to give Sasha and Marina a ride home?" he asked.

Nancy was miffed that he was keeping the game up, but she couldn't say no to him. Their house was close, so she didn't need the car to get home. "No problem," she answered.

"Great. I'll see you in a while, okay?"

"Fine," Nancy said, forcing a careless smile. "Don't get lost."

"I won't." He laughed and went to the car.

"This thing with Ned is really rattling you, isn't it?" George asked as they walked home.

"It is," Nancy admitted. "But worrying about it isn't doing me any good. So I'm just going to concentrate on the case, and let my love life take care of itself."

When they got home, the phone was ringing. Nancy ran over and picked it up. "Hello?"

"Hi, Nancy, it's Ann Granger," a voice said. "I just got your message. What's up?"

"Ann! Fantastic timing," Nancy exclaimed. "I need your investigative-reporter skills." She quickly outlined the case to the reporter, and explained that she was looking for any scandals in Lyons's past. "I think his old business was in San Diego," she concluded. "Can you see what you can find out through the San Diego newspapers?"

"I'll get on it right away and call you back within an hour," Ann promised.

"Terrific." Nancy thanked Ann and hung up. She turned to her friends. "Now we wait."

For the next hour Nancy waited for Ann's call and tried to ignore the fact that Ned wasn't back yet. Finally the phone rang again.

"I don't know if any of this is relevant," came Ann's voice, "but I could find only two things that seemed even vaguely helpful."

"Shoot." Nancy reached for paper and pencil.

"Okay. Roland Lyons and his partner, Craig Berry, owned a construction company in San Diego. It was investigated when two buildings that Lyons and Berry had built collapsed in a minor earthquake. One of the subcontractors was convicted of fraud. Apparently he ignored some safety codes and pocketed the money he should have spent on extra materials. But Lyons and Berry's firm itself was never connected with the fraud."

"Hmm." Nancy didn't think that would have swayed the community board. "What's the second thing?" The front door opened and Ned came in.

The reporter continued, "It's connected. Bill Walters, a reporter who covered the investigation, wrote an editorial— Hey, wait a minute, that's pretty unusual. Reporters don't usually write editorials about their own stories. Well, anyway, this Walters implied that there was more to the case than was made public. He hinted that there was a cover-up, that Lyons paid someone off in city administration."

"That sounds promising," Nancy said excitedly. "Ann, you're terrific. Thanks!"

"Anytime." Ann chuckled and hung up.

Next Nancy tried the San Diego paper that Bill Walters had written for. No one seemed to know who he was. Finally Nancy dialed information and got the reporter's home number. He wasn't in, but she left a message on his answering machine.

"What's going on?" Ned asked. "New lead?"

Nancy brought Ned up-to-date. Then she told them all what Ann had found out. "If this Bill Walters can give us definite information, we're in business," she said, pacing the living room as she thought aloud. "The community board would have refused Lyons the contract if they'd known he had been investigated for fraud. If he thought Emily was on his case, he'd want to keep her quiet until after the contract was signed."

"Assuming you're right about Lyons planning the crime, it seems awfully convenient that the only person who could incriminate him isn't in any shape to answer questions," Ned said slowly.

"You mean Keith?" Nancy looked at Ned in dawning horror. "Ned, what are you saying?"

"Didn't you say Keith ran out of brake fluid?" Ned asked. "That practically never happens, not if you take care of your car."

"And Keith loved his car," Nancy whispered. "I did think it was strange that he would have let that happen. Ned, could you empty a car of brake fluid and make it look accidental?"

Ned shrugged. "Sure. All you'd have to do is unscrew the drain valve. It's right by the wheel— it wouldn't be hard."

"Let's go to the garage and have a look." Nancy was already at the front door.

All four of them raced to the repair shop. Hurrying past the startled mechanic, they ran to the car. Ned crawled under the body and checked out the valve.

When he slid back out, his face was grim. "It's wide open," he reported.

Nancy felt a flutter of horror. It looked as if she'd have to add attempted murder to the list of Lyons's crimes!

Chapter

Sixteen

NANCY TOOK A DEEP BREATH. "It's time to call the police," she said. "If you're right, Ned, we're dealing with attempted murder."

Bess nodded emphatically. "If you don't call them, I will," she said. She was pale.

As they drove home, Nancy had a sudden thought. "Ned, did you touch anything under there?" she asked anxiously. If there were any fingerprints on the valve, he might have messed them up.

Ned shook his head. "No, I was careful. I'd hate for the police to find *my* prints there."

That possibility hadn't even occurred to Nancy. "You'd make a good criminal," she told Ned, smiling.

"It comes from hanging around with you," he said, teasing her back.

Nancy's heart lifted at his affectionate tone. Maybe the deep-freeze treatment was over!

Eloise Drew was home when they got back. George, Bess, and Ned brought her up-to-date while Nancy dialed the police in Montauk.

She told the desk sergeant about the open brake valve on Keith's car, and her suspicions regarding his involvement in Emily's kidnapping.

"These are very serious charges you're making, young lady. Do you have any proof for your allegations?" the sergeant demanded.

"Please, just look at that valve," Nancy begged. "Surely it'll prove someone tried to kill Keith."

"Valves can work loose by themselves," the sergeant told her. "But I'll send someone over to dust for prints in the morning. I don't have anyone available right now."

Well, the car wouldn't go anywhere overnight, Nancy reflected. She looked at her watch. It was almost seven o'clock. Morning was good enough.

She joined everyone else in the kitchen. Her aunt Eloise had made a big bowl of popcorn and some lemonade, and they were all eating popcorn instead of dinner.

"Do you really think Roland Lyons is cold-blooded enough to have tried to kill Keith, just to make sure he didn't talk?" Eloise asked.

"A multimillion-dollar deal is pretty high stakes," George said darkly.

Nancy had thought of something else. "Let's say Lyons offered Keith money to kidnap Emily, but after he'd done it, Keith asked for more—like a percentage of the condo deal, maybe," she suggested. "I bet that's probably what happened. Keith called to quit his job Monday morning, presumably after he'd set Emily adrift. I'll bet that if we checked with the phone company, we'd find out that that call was made from Lyons's house. Keith went there and threatened Lyons, so Lyons decided to get rid of him. He probably unscrewed the valve while Keith was calling Mr. Engel."

Bess shivered. "That's pretty cold-blooded, if you ask me."

"Nancy, how are you going to prove any of this?" her aunt asked. "Your theory sounds reasonable, but it's all guesswork at this point."

"I know. I'm working on it," Nancy replied.

"Not that this isn't interesting, but I'm wiped out," Ned spoke up. He rose from the table with an enormous yawn. "I know it's ridiculously early, but I've got to go to sleep. Good night, everyone."

"Good night," Bess, George, and Eloise chorused.

Nancy tried to join in, but the words stuck in her throat. She was disappointed and hurt. All day she had been waiting to speak to Ned alone, and now that things had finally calmed down and a quiet conversation might have been possible, he was going to bed—without even giving her a good-night kiss!

Oh, grow up, Drew, she scolded herself. She was acting like a spoiled little girl. After all, she had really put Ned in a tough position. She couldn't expect him to forget his own hurt so easily.

No, if she wanted to patch up their relationship, she was going to have to meet Ned halfway —or more than halfway. She'd have to make the first move. It was scary, but now she knew what she wanted, and what she had to do to get it.

The next morning, while her friends went to the beach, Nancy made two calls. First she updated Emily on what she'd found out so far. Then, at eleven, she called Bill Walters again. It would be eight o'clock in San Diego. She didn't want to wake him, but she wanted to make sure she caught him before he went to work.

He answered immediately, and Nancy could sense his excitement before she'd even finished explaining why she was calling.

"Sure I remember that story," he said with a short laugh. "That was the one that changed my career. How could I forget?"

As Walters spoke, Nancy gradually stopped taking notes. She was too engrossed in what he was saying. It seemed that he had uncovered some correspondence that definitely linked Lyons to the safety-violations fraud.

"And it wasn't just that one site, where the two buildings collapsed," Walters told Nancy. "Lyons and Rickenbacker—he's the subcontractor who was convicted—had a whole scam going. I'm certain they built at least a dozen buildings in southern California that didn't meet safety-code requirements. No one knows about those other buildings because none have collapsed yet. But they probably will, sooner or later."

"Wow! Why didn't any of this ever come out?" Nancy asked.

"High-level hush-up." The reporter's voice was bitter. "Lyons must have had someone in the mayor's office on his payroll, because when I started looking into the case, my editor in chief told me to lay off. When I refused, I got fired."

So that was what Walters had meant about changing his career. Poor guy!

"How much do you think Lyons made in illegal profits?" Nancy asked.

"Close to a million," Walters replied promptly. "But during the investigation I think he had to pay a lot of it out in bribes. When he left the state, I don't think he took more than a few hundred thousand dollars with him. Enough to get himself a new life and a new career on the East Coast, but not much more."

"Why did he leave?" Nancy asked.

"Berry forced him out, I think. Berry wasn't in

131

on the scam, and my guess is that he found out about Lyons. Berry didn't want to risk a scandal, so he didn't turn Lyons in, but I think he more or less forced Lyons to leave."

Nancy had one final question. "Can you prove any of this?" she asked.

Walters hesitated. "Not beyond the shadow of a doubt," he said at last, "but the circumstantial evidence is convincing. I could make a good case."

"Thanks, Mr. Walters," Nancy said fervently.

No sooner had she hung up than the telephone rang. Nancy picked it up.

"Nancy, it's Sasha. Can we talk?"

Sasha! Guiltily Nancy realized that she had barely even thought about him in the past twenty-four hours.

Well, as painful as the discussion would be, she had to go through with it. She had to tell him she wasn't in love with him.

They arranged to meet at Nino's diner in half an hour. As she drove into town, Nancy thought about what she would say to Sasha. They were too different. . . . Ned and she had something very special. . . . Sasha shouldn't base his career decisions on anybody but himself. . . .

She went into the diner with flutters in her stomach. Sasha was already waiting in a booth. He looks nervous, too, Nancy thought. I wonder if he knows what I'm going to say?

"I ordered you a soda," Sasha said as she sat

down opposite him in the booth. "I have something to tell you."

"What?" Nancy asked, surprised.

Sasha gazed into his water glass. "I hope you will not be hurt, but—I have decided to stop chasing you."

"What did you say?" Nancy was so surprised she nearly choked on her soda.

"I won't chase you anymore," Sasha repeated. He leaned forward, frowning earnestly. "I do not think I should base a career decision on anyone but myself. I cannot get the training I need here. And I don't think you and I are really suited to each other. We are very different."

Nancy leaned back against the plastic seat, shaken. How had this happened? She had come there prepared to break Sasha's heart, and instead he was breaking hers!

"So that's it?" she managed to get out. "That's all you have to say?"

Sasha hesitated a moment. Then he shook his head. "No," he said quietly. "I was going to leave it that way, but I cannot. The truth is, I already know your heart. If you felt about me the way I feel about you, you would have made up your mind long ago."

Nancy looked down at the table, tracing a pattern on the Formica with her straw. He was right, but the truth hurt nonetheless. She nodded, not trusting her voice to speak.

"When Ned got here," Sasha continued, "it

was too hard for me. I could see the way you felt about him. I like Ned. He is a fine person. And I didn't want to compete with him—especially because I knew I would lose. I am not used to losing, Nancy. I don't like it. So I think I will bow out now, before it gets any more painful."

"Oh, Sasha." Nancy felt tears brimming in her eyes. "I'm so sorry."

He gave her that familiar slow smile. His blue eyes were extra bright as he said, "So am I."

Nancy fumbled for her bag. She could barely see through the haze of tears. "I guess I'd better go," she murmured. She rose.

His voice stopped her at the door. "Nancy?"

"Yes?" Nancy said, turning.

"What's happening with the case?"

Nancy stared at him. "The case?"

"Yes. You know, Emily's kidnapping. Have you got any new leads?"

A smile stole across Nancy's face. So Sasha still wanted to be friends. Well, that was fine with her. Just fine!

"New leads? Are you kidding?" she exclaimed, heading back to the table. "Wait till you hear!"

After discussing the case with Sasha, Nancy headed home. She felt a little sad, but she knew her decision about Sasha had been the right one. *Our* decision, she corrected herself. It had been Sasha's, too. Now all that remained was to patch things up with Ned. And she was going to do that as soon as possible.

A piece of paper was pinned to the front door of the house. It was addressed to Nancy. Wondering, she turned it over. A note was scrawled on the other side.

"Nancy," it read, "I'm going to Smithson's shed. Please meet me there—it's urgent! I'll explain when I see you. Must run. Emily."

What could it be about? Nancy mused as she got back into her car and drove to the shed. Emily's car was already there. Nancy jumped out of her car and slammed the door. "Emily?" she called.

There was no answer. Feeling somehow uneasy, Nancy hurried into the dark shed. It was empty except for a medium-size powerboat bobbing at the dock. Where did that come from? she wondered.

She stepped forward. "Emily?" she said again.

Too late, she heard a sound behind her. Before she could turn, an arm snaked around her throat. She opened her mouth to scream, but instead gasped with surprise as a piece of wet gauze was slapped over her mouth. She smelled the sickly sweet odor of chloroform.

And then the world went black.

Chapter

Seventeen

Nancy's eyes fluttered open slowly. Where am I? she wondered. The ground seemed to be rocking under her. There was something covering her mouth. She tried to reach up to remove it, but both her hands were bound behind her. She was a prisoner!

In a flash she remembered the arm around her throat in the darkness of the boat shed and the smell of chloroform. She must be in the cabin of the powerboat that had been docked there.

Rolling her head to the side, Nancy squinted in the dimness. Her eyes widened. Emily lay on the bunk across from Nancy's. She was bound and gagged, as Nancy was. She appeared to be unconscious.

136

Lyons must be behind this, Nancy guessed. He must have written that note to lure me here. But how did he know we were onto him?

She tensed as she heard the hatch opening. Across from her, Emily moaned. She was coming to.

The hatch opened, and Roland Lyons appeared. He snapped on the light and gazed down at his two captives, frowning as if the sight of them annoyed him. Lyons wasn't looking his usual dapper self, either. His suit was rumpled, and his horn-rimmed glasses were askew on his nose.

"Good morning, ladies," he said briskly. "Or should I say good evening? It's dusk, you know. You both slept the day away.

"You're causing me a lot of trouble," he continued. "Especially you, Emily. I don't like trouble. So I've decided to dispose of you both."

At his words, Nancy felt a thrill of fear. She strained against her bonds.

"Don't bother," Lyons told her with a smug smile. "I'm good at knots. You look like you want to say something. I'll remove your gag if you promise not to scream or anything. If you scream, I'll get very annoyed. Do you promise?"

Nancy nodded reluctantly. She had no choice.

Lyons pulled the strip of tape off her mouth. "Sensible girl," he said. "If only you'd been a little *more* sensible earlier and minded your own business, we wouldn't be in this position now.

It's unpleasant for me, too, you know. I don't want to kill you—but you're forcing me to."

Nancy had to stall him somehow while she thought of a way out of this mess.

"Why kidnap Emily in the first place?" she questioned. "She was no real threat to you."

"What do you mean?" Lyons retorted. "She was hot on my trail! She'd talked to Berry, she already knew about the earthquake and the building collapsing. It was only a matter of time before she found out the rest."

"But she *didn't* know," Nancy told him, confused. "Your old partner wouldn't tell her anything. We didn't find out about the earthquake until yesterday afternoon."

"Don't pull that on me. I heard you talking in the diner," Lyons said angrily. "You were all whispering, and then somebody shrieked, 'Earthquake!' Why are you playing dumb now?"

"So that's why," Nancy whispered as the truth hit her. She remembered George's comment about earthquakes and Bess's squealed response. Lyons had heard and had thought they were talking about his guilty secret.

It had all been a horrible misunderstanding!

She shook her head. "We didn't know anything until yesterday," she told Lyons wearily.

"Oh, really?" Lyons sounded bored. "Well, it's too bad I went to all this trouble. You know now, so you've got to be taken care of." He started for the hatch.

"Wait!" Nancy cried. Lyons turned. "How did you find out *I* knew about you?" she asked.

"Thank your crusading friend here," Lyons answered, hooking a thumb over his shoulder at Emily. The girl stared back at Nancy, imploring forgiveness with her eyes.

"I was working at home today," Lyons went on, "and it's a good thing I was, because Emily came storming over, vowing to bring me to justice. The stupid girl thought she could gloat over me before calling in the police."

Lyons chuckled briefly. "I let her talk until I found out where she'd gotten her information and then I tapped her on the head and brought her here. It was easy to write the note to you. I gambled that even if you knew what Emily's handwriting looked like, you wouldn't notice the note was a fake. You'd just think she was in a rush."

"Smart," Nancy murmured.

"Of course it was smart. I didn't get where I am by being stupid," Lyons boasted.

"What are you going to do with us?" Nancy asked, ignoring his boast.

Lyons smirked. "It's another brilliant plan, if I do say so myself. You're going for a joyride, girls. This boat, the *Marlene*, belongs to my neighbor, who's out of town for the month. And everyone knows Emily Terner is a wild girl. I can hear the gossip now. Naughty Emily—she talked that nice Nancy Drew into 'borrowing' Roger Lindsay's powerboat for a little adventure on the open ocean. And then something went wrong with the fuel line, and the boat blew up. Such a tragedy! Such lovely girls!" He heaved a theatrical sigh.

"Very clever," Nancy said sarcastically. She didn't want him to see her worry. But she also thought she might have found a flaw in his plan.

"I have a question," she continued. "How do you plan to force us to drive the boat? You can't do it yourself—remember your seasickness?"

"If I hadn't taken care of that, I wouldn't be here now," Lyons said, whipping out a little plastic case with a flourish. He extracted two flat patches. "I've got a cure! These patches are new on the market. You stick them behind your ears, and they release a drug that seeps into your skin and neutralizes the vertigo. Isn't science wonderful?" he added, beaming.

"Terrific." Nancy couldn't keep the tremor out of her voice anymore. She was scared.

"I used to love boating, before I damaged my ears," Lyons told her. "But enough about me. Back to what I'm going to do with you.

"When I get out a suitable distance, I'm going to plug the electric starter wand from my grill into the cockpit outlet. Then I'm going to lay it against the inboard motor's fuel line. In a few minutes, it will melt through the rubber and ignite the fuel inside. And when that happens"— he threw his hands wide—"boom! I, of course, will be safely away in my motorized dinghy. But I'll be watching." He grinned.

140

"You can't get away with this," Nancy warned. "I already told the police about you."

Lyons looked worried, but then he laughed. "You're bluffing. If you'd told the police, they'd have come after me by now." He turned to go.

"I told my friends. It's the truth. You've lost!" Nancy called after him. But he didn't stop. He didn't believe her! Nancy sagged. Even though it was true that her friends knew about Lyons's past, that wouldn't help her or Emily now.

"Nancy," Emily whispered. She had worked her gag off. "What are we going to do?"

She sounded close to panic. Nancy shook her head. "I don't know, but we'll think of something," she promised. She doubled up her legs and tried to work her bound hands over them. If she could get her hands in front of her, she might be able to do something with the radio.

There was a roar as Lyons started the boat's powerful engine. Emily began to cry. Nancy redoubled her efforts. Time was running out!

Finally she gave up. She'd have to do it with her hands behind her. Swinging her bound legs down to the floor, she hopped over to the communications console. "Stop crying," she told Emily. "We're going to make it!"

Nancy flipped the on-off switch with her mouth. Then she looked for a microphone. She'd have to trust the thing was on the right frequency —she had no idea how to change it if it wasn't.

Then she gasped in horror. The microphone

was gone! Where it should have been, there were only two bare wires.

"I cut it off," Lyons's voice came from behind her. She turned. He was peering in through the hatch. "I know you're a resourceful girl—I thought you might try something like this." He smiled pleasantly at her and disappeared.

Emily let out a sob. Nancy swallowed hard. She felt like crying herself.

What else could they do? In desperation, Nancy groped for the exposed wires with her bound hands behind her. She touched the ends together. There was a crackle.

They were live! Nancy felt a flare of hope. Maybe she could send a message in Morse code!

"SOS," she tapped. Short—long—short. "SOS." It was hard with her hands behind her back. The wires gave her tiny pinprick shocks every time she touched them together, but she kept on.

She tapped out all the information she could think of: the name of the boat, the location they'd left from, and their rough heading—east, toward the open sea. She repeated these twice. Then she went back to the SOS.

After about fifteen minutes she gave it up and hopped over to Emily. "Sit up," she said urgently. "We've got to get our hands and legs untied. You work on my hands, I'll do yours."

For ten minutes the girls pulled frantically at each other's bonds. Then came the sound Nancy had been dreading. The *Marlene*'s engine slowed to a throbbing idle as the boat came to a halt.

Lyons stuck his head through the hatch again. "All systems are go!" he announced brightly. "I'm off. I'll say my goodbyes now, since I won't see you later, I'm afraid." Then he was gone. Nancy heard the dinghy putt-putt away.

"Don't stop trying!" she told Emily fiercely. "You're almost loose. We still have a chance!"

They worked for a minute or two more. Suddenly Emily gave a triumphant cry.

"I think I can get my hand out—there!" Nancy felt her wrench it free. Then she turned and fumbled at Nancy's wrists.

"There!" Emily cried as the knots parted. "Now for our legs."

"No! No time," Nancy said breathlessly. She grabbed Emily's hand and dragged her to the hatch. "Pull yourself up," she directed.

The girls hauled themselves up through the hatch and out onto the dark deck. Nancy looked around, but she couldn't see where Lyons had placed the electric starter wand. She made a split-second decision. "We'll have to swim for it!"

Emily nodded wordlessly, and the two girls hopped to the rail. Nancy threw herself over, and felt cold, black sea water close around her. A splash beside her told her that Emily had done the same.

They swam away from the *Marlene* as quickly

as they could, using only their arms. Nancy could feel the strain already—she tried not to think about how far out to sea they might be.

After a few minutes Nancy heard a new noise: the throb of a big boat's engine. Peering to her left, she saw in the faint moonlight the dark bulk of a ship about a hundred yards away. Overjoyed, she waved an arm in the air. "Help!" she screamed.

A powerful beam of light cut the night, blinding Nancy as it swept over her. A voice boomed, "This is the coast guard! Ahoy, there—are you in trouble?"

The coast guard! Thank goodness! Nancy continued to wave her arms. "Help!" she repeated.

The boat chugged closer, and then a life preserver landed in the water near Nancy. She snatched it and was pulled through the water and aboard the cutter, Emily beside her.

"Get away from that boat! Now!" Nancy shouted at the captain as soon as she could speak.

He didn't ask questions. He just threw the cutter into reverse. "Full speed astern!"

Nancy gazed tensely at the receding boat. They'd barely gone a hundred yards when a tremendous blast shook the night. The *Marlene* disappeared in an explosive cloud of fire.

Feeling suddenly faint, Nancy swayed and clutched at the rail. It was over.

Chapter

Eighteen

THE REST OF THE NIGHT passed in a blur. The coast-guard captain radioed to the police, and when they pulled into the harbor at Montauk, a squad car was waiting for Nancy and Emily.

At the police station a grizzled, solid-looking man in a rumpled suit came forward. "My name's Mayer," he said. "I'm a detective. Why don't you tell me exactly what happened?"

Detective Mayer led them to his office and took their statements. Nancy explained how she'd come to believe that Roland Lyons and Keith Artin had plotted Emily's abduction, and how she thought Lyons had tried to kill Keith. Then she and Emily together told the detective about how Lyons had attempted to kill them.

"I sent a car out to pick him up after I first spoke to the coast guard," Detective Mayer told them. He peered through the open door. "In fact, I think I see the officers bringing him in now. Come with me."

Wondering, Nancy and Emily followed Mayer out into the main area of the police station. He walked right up to Lyons, who was sitting on a bench, studying his nails.

"Mr. Lyons," said Detective Mayer, "do you recognize these two girls?"

Lyons looked up. His face turned almost gray. Maybe he thinks he's seeing ghosts, Nancy guessed. He left us for dead.

"Hello, Mr. Lyons," she said quietly.

After that he broke down. He was making a confession when Detective Mayer led the girls back to his office. Mayer turned to Nancy.

"By the way, thanks for your call yesterday, Ms. Drew," he said. "We did dust for prints on the underbody of Keith Artin's car. We found a couple around the brake valve that we couldn't identify, but I suspect that when we get prints on our friend Roland Lyons, they'll match up. I guess he didn't have time to put on a pair of gloves when he was rigging the brakes that day."

Nancy shuddered. "He certainly is cold-blooded," she commented.

Mayer nodded grimly. "We'll put him away, don't worry. I understand Keith Artin is conscious now, so we can get a statement from him, too. I think he'll talk when he hears how Lyons tried to kill him."

"I guess the condo deal will be scrapped if Lyons goes to jail, huh?" Emily asked hopefully.

Mayer shrugged. "I imagine so. Lyons can't very well conduct his business from behind bars," he replied.

A police officer stuck her head into the office. "A Mr. Nickerson and a Mr. Terner are here to pick up these girls," she announced.

"Dad!" Emily shot out of her chair. "He must have been frantic. He's such a worrier!"

Nancy followed Emily out, grinning. Relations between Emily and her father were definitely getting better.

Then Nancy saw Ned and ran into his arms. "Oh, Ned," she murmured. "I was afraid I'd never see you again."

"Shhh," he whispered, stroking her hair. "Don't talk now. Come on, let's go home."

"Go, Emily! Come on, *Swallow!*" George cried. She clutched Nancy's arm in her excitement.

"You can do it, Tommy and Seth!" Bess called. She grabbed Nancy's other arm. "Isn't this fun?" she exclaimed.

Nancy grinned. "Ow! Take it easy," she begged. "My arms haven't recovered from their big workout last night."

It was a cloudless, windy Saturday, the day of

the big regatta. This was a five-race series, and four of the races were already finished. Seth Cooper and Emily Terner had each won two, splitting the series evenly. This final race would determine who took the trophy home this year.

Nancy didn't know whom to root for, Seth or Emily. Emily was her friend, but she liked Seth a lot, and he *was* her aunt Eloise's boyfriend. If things kept going so well between them, he might even be part of the family one day! she thought with a grin.

Finally she decided that no matter who won, she'd be happy. It was much easier that way.

Emily and Seth were flying toward the finish line now, and it was impossible to tell who was winning. Both were sailing wing-and-wing. Tommy stood on the foredeck of the *Twice Shy*, holding out the jib with a long pole to get the most wind possible, and Emily's crewman was doing the same.

Both boats sailed past the final mark, and Nancy still couldn't tell who had been in the lead. There were a few moments of silence, and then the judge's voice boomed out.

"And the winner of this year's trophy is Seth Cooper!" the judge declared.

Bess jumped up and down, shrieking with joy. "They won! They did it!" she kept saying. "Oh, I'm so proud of Tommy."

"Isn't it wonderful?" Eloise put in. She was standing next to Bess, glowing with pleasure. "Seth will be so happy!"

Nancy stepped apart from her friends and scanned the bleachers for Ned, but she couldn't spot him. She frowned. She still hadn't had a chance to tell him about her discussion with Sasha. Ever since she'd come back from her adventure the night before, she hadn't had a moment to herself. She'd been besieged by calls from the police, reporters, and well-wishers all morning.

"Are you looking for Ned?" a familiar voice said in her ear. "He just hitched a ride from Dmitri. He asked me to tell you he'd be at home."

It was Sasha. Nancy stared at him, puzzled. "At home?" she repeated. "Why did he leave?"

Sasha shrugged. "He didn't tell me."

Uneasy, Nancy headed for her car. Was Ned feeling ill? Or was he upset about something?

Nancy's puzzlement grew when she got home and found the place empty. Then she spotted a note on the kitchen table.

"Meet me at the beach," it said. It was unsigned, but Nancy recognized Ned's writing.

Wondering, Nancy went down the deck stairs and through the dune grass to the beach.

"I thought it was time we talked," Ned's voice said from behind her. She turned. He was sitting by a steep dune, his face unreadable.

Nancy suddenly felt at a loss for words. She sat down beside him and let the wind whip her red-blond hair around her face. "Ned, I—" she began after a moment.

"I want to apologize for the way I've been acting," he interrupted. His voice was gruff. "I know I've been a jerk. But I was so—so torn apart at the idea that I might be losing you. It made me crazy!"

Nancy hadn't expected this. "Ned," she said, facing him, "why are you apologizing to *me?* I'm the one who should be saying I'm sorry. You're the most wonderful guy in the world, and I was almost dumb enough to let you go. I should have my head examined!"

"I've just been kicking myself for not handling the whole situation better, especially since that day when my stupid need to show off nearly got Sasha killed," Ned said. Then he looked up sharply at Nancy, as if her words had just penetrated. "What did you say?" he asked.

"I said I should have my head examined," Nancy repeated. "I don't want to break up with you, Ned. You're too much a part of me."

Ned took her face between his hands and looked her in the eye. "And what about Sasha?" he asked quietly.

"Out of the picture, by mutual agreement," Nancy told him. "Sasha is—too different. And Sasha isn't *you*, Ned Nickerson."

"I'll agree with you there," Ned said, a slow grin stealing across his face. "But you said something else—something about me being a pretty great guy?"

Nancy laughed softly at him and leaned forward to slide her arms around his neck. It felt so right to be with him like this. How could she ever have forgotten, even for a moment?

"I said that you're the most wonderful guy in the world. And I think I'm hopelessly in love with you," she murmured in his ear.

"Hopelessly, huh? Well, I hate to see you hopeless, so I'll tell you a secret." Ned kissed her nose lightly, his eyes glowing. "I'm hopelessly in love with you, too."

And then Ned's lips met hers, and Nancy lost herself in the wonderful, warm, tingling feeling that bubbled up inside her.

When Ned drew back, Nancy smiled radiantly at him. The sun was shining, the breeze was blowing, she had solved a complicated case, and she was in the arms of the guy she loved.

Life was just about perfect!

Nancy's next case:

A major modeling agency, a designer clothes company, and a popular teen magazine promise to make one girl's dreams come true. All are sponsors of the Face of the Year contest—and Bess is a finalist! With Nancy at her side, she's off to Chicago to seek the fame and fortune that await the winner.

But the competition is fierce, and deceit proves to be the hottest fashion of all. A desperate campaign of dirty tricks has brought the contest face-to-face with disaster and scandal—and the spotlight falls on Nancy as she tries to unmask the cover girl cover-up . . . in *A MODEL CRIME*, Case #51 in the Nancy Drew Files℠.

Forthcoming Titles in the
Nancy Drew Files™ Series

Simon & Schuster publish a wide range of titles from pre-school books to books for adults.

For up-to-date catalogues, please contact:

International Book Distributors
Campus 400
Maylands Avenue
Hemel Hempstead
Herts
HP2 7EZ

Tel. 0442 882255